BUNYIPS AND BILLABONGS

BUNYIPS AND BILLABONGS

PENNY AND BOOTS™ BOOK FOUR

AMY HOPKINS

MICHAEL ANDERLE

This book is a work of fiction. All of the characters, organizations, and events portrayed in this novel are either products of the author's imagination or are used fictitiously. Sometimes both.

Copyright © 2020 Amy Hopkins & Michael T. Anderle
Cover by Fantasy Book Design
Cover copyright © LMBPN Publishing
This book is a Michael Anderle Production

LMBPN Publishing supports the right to free expression and the value of copyright. The purpose of copyright is to encourage writers and artists to produce the creative works that enrich our culture.

The distribution of this book without permission is a theft of the author's intellectual property. If you would like permission to use material from the book (other than for review purposes), please contact support@lmbpn.com. Thank you for your support of the author's rights.

LMBPN Publishing
PMB 196, 2540 South Maryland Pkwy
Las Vegas, NV 89109

First US edition, April 2020
eBook ISBN: 978-1-64202-836-2
Print ISBN: 978-1-64202-837-9

THE BUNYIPS AND BILLABONGS TEAM

Thanks to the JIT Readers

Dave Hicks
Kathleen Fettig
Jackey Hankard-Brodie
Diane L. Smith
Veronica Stephan-Miller
DebMader
Larry Omans
Angel LaVey
Debi Sateren

If I've missed anyone, please let me know!

Editor
SkyHunter Editing Team

To Peanut Butter. Thank you for being the cutest fluff I've ever seen. For the last eight months you've been a companion, support pupper, hole-digging-helper and inefficient babysitter. I love you, boy. Sorry for getting your balls cut off.

— Amy

To Family, Friends and
Those Who Love
to Read.
May We All Enjoy Grace
to Live the Life We Are
Called.

— Michael

"It's almost time to land, folks. Can I take your glasses?" The flight attendant, Heath, flounced over to Cisco with a gratuitous wink. "How about yours, love?"

Cisco passed Heath his empty cup, laughing. "Does that mean we have to say goodbye?"

"Sure does, hot stuff." Heath leaned across Cisco to accept the glass Penny offered him with a grin. "Woah, sweetheart. That mojito was a double, right? Don't you let that go to your head, now."

Penny smirked. "I can handle my booze."

"Spoken like a true local." Heath shrugged, then cleared off the small table in front of Red's and Amelia's seats.

The long flight had been made enjoyable not just by Heath, the flamboyant Australian attendant, but by all the creature comforts offered by Mack's private plane. It was understated but comfortable and had enough room for the six of them to spread out. Not that Boots needed much room. Enamored of Heath and his fawning adoration, she'd spent most of the flight draped over his shoulders like a giant feather boa, just without the feathers.

"Now, remember what I told you about the landing procedure?" Heath asked, hands on his hips. Boots lifted her head off his chest to nod. "We wait for the ground sweepers to get rid of the nasty biteys, then we hightail it outta there like we're being chased by snakes. Because we will be."

Cisco gripped Penny's hand, and she shot him an amused glance. "Not scared, are you?" she asked.

He shook his head but stopped when she caught his eye. "Look, I'm okay with snakes," he explained. "But...this is *Australia*, and they're Mythers."

"And that's exactly why it's an issue," Heath said with a groan. "Bloody tourists. Snakes this, and spiders that. It's nothing a solid boot to the head won't fix!"

"Americans are crazy." Penny ducked a glare from Amelia. "I mean, come on. I know my country. You're way more likely to get king-hit by a guy named Dane in a Bintang singlet than bitten by a damn snake."

"Translation?" Red asked, turning a quizzical face to Heath.

"She means you're more likely to get punched in the face by an asshole than bitten by a spider." Heath grinned at Penny. "She's not wrong."

A nearby speaker dinged, and the pilot's voice rang out over the intercom. "Landing in five, guys."

"Right! Strap in. Or strap on, whatever you prefer." Heath sauntered to his seat and buckled the belt. "Going down is my favorite part."

"Where does Mack find these people?" Cisco murmured to Penny as the plane began its descent.

Penny watched out the window as the scattered reptiles on the tarmac below lifted their heads. As the plane touched down, they slithered toward it, moving with eerie speed as they coalesced into a writhing mass. The wheels shuddered over the bumps, and Penny wondered how many Myther snakes they'd just turned into roadkill.

"I like the lad," Red stated with a grin. The flattery Heath had heaped on the two men certainly hadn't hurt his case, although Cisco seemed less swayed by it than Red.

Heath slipped into his professional persona. "Ladies and Gentlemen, welcome to Sydney Airport. For your safety and comfort, please remain seated while the runway is cleared. This should only take a few minutes."

Penny glanced outside again as Heath rattled off the safety instructions. When she had flown out of Australia, the airport had still been struggling with the influx of Myther snakes —byproducts of a worldwide belief that no matter where you stepped in Australia, a giant snake or spider would be ready to eat you whole.

The tightly-held conviction had brought a steady stream of the creatures through the Veil, most of them concentrating in the places terrified tourists congregated: the airports.

Penny was impressed by the efficiency of the ground sweepers—the newly-coined term for those whose job it was to clear the incursion. Several trucks had already rolled toward the plane, and the ground sweepers riding them had their fat hoses directed at the ground. In perfect unison, they blasted the tarmac with jets of water, carefully sweeping the hoses from side to side to wash away the creatures.

The entire operation only took a few minutes. When Heath unclipped his seatbelt and stood, Penny did the same. Boots finally wriggled away from her new friend and slithered back to Penny.

"It'll take you all day to get her through Customs," Heath warned. "If you want to skip the mountain of paperwork, you'd better do your thing here."

"Oh, right." Penny slipped a small flask from her pocket and unscrewed the lid. Boots hissed at Heath, then nosed the mouth of the bottle. When Penny gently tipped it so the water met the lip, and Boots flicked her tail and dove in, only to pop out a moment later, having shrunk down to a thin rope the width of Penny's little finger. The newly tiny Boots lunged up to kiss Heath on the cheek.

"Aww. She's so precious." Heath waved at the flask as Boots disappeared back into it. With a regretful sigh, he ushered the others toward the door. "Okay, folks. Your bags will be coming along shortly. For now, it's a quick disembark and then hustle to the building. You should be safe once you're inside."

Red and Amelia shot out and took off running across the tarmac. Cisco gave Penny a pained look.

"Oh, for God's sake. Go!" She waved him away, then turned to Heath to say goodbye. "Thanks for the fun ride, mate, and tell Mack we owe him for the trip."

"You're *sure* your man doesn't have a brother?" Heath asked with a sly wink.

"Sorry." Penny leaned in to give him a spontaneous hug. "Have a safe flight back, mate."

He returned her embrace with feeling. "You too, babe!"

Heath stepped back, and Penny moved onto the top step. The heat had already begun to filter into the crisp chill of the plane, but standing in the full sun, Penny bore the brunt.

She sucked in a breath. The baking heat gave her a prickle of familiarity, a deep comfort that itched against the knowledge that, though she was about to step foot in her homeland, it wouldn't be for long. *I'm home.* She jogged down the steps to catch up with her friends, then slowed. *Screw that. It's too hot to run.*

The path to the airport was lined with more ground crew standing several feet apart, each holding an oversized knife pointed toward the writhing, snapping snakes that had already begun to swarm back onto the runway.

"What is that?" Penny asked one of them, noticing that the knives seemed to hold power over the reptiles.

The man she had approached flashed her a brilliant grin. "It's not just a knife, love."

The reference hit her instantly. "It's a *knife*, right?" She shook her head in disbelief. None of her classes at the Academy had mentioned this little gem of information. "Since when does Croc Dundee ward off snakes?"

The man shrugged. "No idea. But can you get a move along? My arm's getting tired, and it's really damn hot out here."

"Sorry, man." Penny picked up her pace and hurried inside.

The taxi ride to the hotel was quiet. Penny had adjusted to the heat almost instantly, although her friends weren't so adaptable. Amelia wilted, despite being in the front with the air con on full. On Penny's left, Red stuck his head as far out of the window as the driver would let him, mouth open and tongue hanging to his chin like an excited puppy. On her right, Cisco kept pulling his damp shirt off his skin, moaning about the horrible weather.

Despite Penny's best efforts to strike up a conversation with them, it fell flat. Eventually, she leaned forward to speak to the driver.

"How's your day been?" she asked.

"Oh, nice enough. Lovely weather. You?" He turned the wheel and cruised around a corner, then reached out to tickle the small monkey on his dash under the chin.

"Nice monkey," Penny said. It reminded her of Boots, who was still securely hidden in the flask. Penny briefly considered freeing the serpent, then considered what would happen if the monkey took fright in the crowded cab. *She won't mind waiting a little longer.* "What's the little guy's name?"

The driver shrugged one shoulder. "I don't know. He's one of those, you know, *Mythers.*"

"Oh?" Penny cocked her head. "I haven't heard about random monkeys appearing."

"The depot told us they come under the 'racial perception' umbrella." He sighed. "Apparently, there are people who think Indians all own pet monkeys. I've never even *been* to India!"

The monkey chittered, then pulled a peanut from behind its back and shelled it, tossing the rubbish on the floor. It nibbled the snack, its big, round eyes glued to Penny.

"That's…" Penny sat back in her seat. "Okay, it's not *quite* as weird as the snakes or the knives."

"Penny, your whole country is weird." Cisco pulled his shirt away from his damp skin yet again. "Weird, and hot."

"Like me?" She lifted a sardonic eyebrow.

"I didn't say that!" Cisco made a half-hearted attempt to duck her swat, but the heat had taken more out of him than she had realized.

"Damn. Do we need to stop and get you guys a cup of concrete?" Penny rolled her eyes when she was met with quizzical looks all around. "Harden up! It's not even summer, for crying out loud. Look, we're almost at the hotel. Once we're there, suck down some hydration, hit the pool, and *try* not to embarrass me in front of my people."

"I seem to remember taking you shopping on your first day at the Academy so you could buy a winter coat in the middle of spring," Amelia pointed out.

"And I appreciated it." Penny grinned. "So much that I'd hug you if you didn't look like a wet rag."

"Ha-ha." Amelia at least mustered up a smile, one that broadened as the cab turned off the street and into the driveway of a hotel. "Huh. It doesn't look like a dive."

"What's the bet Mack's paying for this?" Cisco asked. "Either that or Crenel's stories about the roach motels the FBI puts him in are lies."

"It's Crenel," Penny pointed out. She leaned across to tug the door handle, pushed Cisco out, and then tumbled out herself. She stopped to stretch her numb limbs. "He'd call the Palazzo Versace a roach motel."

"Fair point." Cisco handed the driver a credit card. "Does he know we're here?"

Penny nodded. "I messaged him when I got in the taxi." She slipped her phone out. "He hasn't responded, though. Maybe he's busy?"

The check-in process was fast and easy, although there was a slight hesitation when the desk attendant handed out keys.

"Here's room nine-nineteen," she told them, sliding two cards across the desk. "And these two are room nine-twenty."

Amelia slipped the first card into her pocket and Penny reached for the one beside it, only to bump hands with Red. Penny raised an eyebrow at Amelia.

"What?" Amelia grabbed the card and passed it to her boyfriend. "We're not on Academy grounds. We're not even in the same country!"

"I didn't say a word!" Penny grinned, grabbed the last two cards, and handed one to Cisco.

CHAPTER TWO

Once they had all freshened up, Penny knocked on the door three down from hers. "I wonder why he didn't just book three rooms in a row?"

Red snorted. "Do you think he wants to hear us humping all night?"

Penny rolled her eyes. "If you keep me up all night with the sound of—"

Cisco cleared his throat and knocked on the door again.

"Coming!" Crenel's voice was muffled.

The door still didn't open. Penny heard his shuffling steps, a faucet, then finally, the beep of the hotel door card. Crenel yanked the door open and glared at them with bleary eyes. "What are you doing here?"

"Briefing?" Penny sighed. "You didn't get my text, did you?"

"That was only five…" Crenel glanced at his watch. "Oh. Must've nodded off again." He yawned and stretched. "I'm too old to deal with jetlag."

Crenel let them wait awkwardly while he washed his

face again, then disappeared into his bathroom to change into an only slightly less-rumpled shirt. He emerged, still ignoring them, and grabbed a protein bar out of his bag.

Meanwhile, Boots explored the room, tugging open drawers, disappearing under his bed, and experimentally twisting the taps on the spa bath by the corner window.

"Boots!" Penny hissed as the bath began to fill. "That's rude!"

"She's fine," Crenel mumbled through a mouthful of his low-carb peanut butter protein bar.

When he was done eating, Agent Crenel tossed a manila folder on the coffee table in front of Penny. The word Confidential was stamped in big red letters across the front.

"This case is a little more complex than what you've dealt with previously. And there's another key difference. This time, we're hunting a human." Crenel slid his cigarettes from his pocket, pulled one out, and tapped it on the box.

"You know you're not allowed to do that in here," Amelia pointed out. "And a human? That's not our specialty. Why us?"

"This case is…complicated. Instead of saving humans from Mythers, we're flipping the script. It's the Mythers that are in danger if we're right." Crenel scowled at Amelia, who was still eyeing his unlit cigarette. "And what are you, my mother?" he snapped.

"No, but your wife is the dean of our school," Amelia retorted. "She told us to keep an eye on you. I'm pretty sure she'll fail us all this semester if we don't keep you out of trouble."

Crenel grunted. "You're a bunch of kids. It's not your job to keep me out of trouble."

Red pointed at the sprinklers on the ceiling. "Look, Agent Crenel. I just got out of the shower. I don't need another one."

"Besides, it'll make my mascara run." Amelia leaned forward and tugged the cigarette and its box out of Crenel's hands. "Now. You were saying?"

Crenel gave a growl of frustration but let the matter drop. "Our target is a man named Geoffrey Nevins. His family has been linked to several crime syndicates over the years, and he himself has a reputation for importing goods of dubious origins."

He flipped the folder open and quickly rifled through the pages, then slid a page toward them. On it was a photograph of a man with striking blue eyes and short blond hair.

"He looks like the villain of a Bruce Willis movie," Cisco commented.

"If he has done what we think he's done, he might as well be." Crenel absentmindedly reached into the pocket his cigarettes had been in, then grimaced. Irritated, he stood up, strode to the minibar, and grabbed a tiny bottle of whiskey.

"You know that's probably going to cost you forty-five dollars?" Amelia asked.

"Jesus Christ, what is my wife bribing you with?" Crenel shoved the bottle back into the minibar and slammed the door. He turned to face Amelia, arms crossed over his chest. "Is there anything *else* you want to complain about?"

Amelia giggled. "Come on, Agent Crenel. You know we're only doing it because we care."

Still scowling, Crenel continued the briefing. "We came close to nabbing Nevins a couple of years ago for his alleged involvement in the ivory trade. We couldn't make it stick, though."

Penny picked up the file Crenel had discarded on the table and began flipping through it. "There are rap sheets for his whole family here. Are we just after this guy, or will there be others involved?"

Crenel shrugged. "At this point, we don't even know if it *is* him. If it is, we believe he will be working alone—or at least, not with his family involved." He took the papers again and shuffled through them, this time pulling out a sheet of typed notes. He read from them, eyes scanning the pages as he picked out the pertinent details.

"The sister was arrested two years ago. She's still serving time. The father died under extremely suspicious circumstances a few years back, but the case was never solved. Nevins' mother has been moved to a nursing home. Her health is failing, and from what I understand, they don't expect her to last much longer. The only other family member listed here is a brother, Silas, but he's off the table."

Penny held her hand out for the page of notes. "What do you mean?"

"He's been in his own trouble. He's one of those vegan terrorists, but not this new wave. He had a few arrests from the nineties: breaking into pig farms, causing trouble at research labs, that sort of thing." Crenel shook his head. "There's every chance that guy is out breaking the law somewhere, but he won't be involved in a Myther poaching ring."

Penny looked up at the agent. Something was bothering her. "Why *us*? I know the bureau is short-staffed, but this is an international case. And a huge one, if all this is right. Surely there must be hundreds of agents, both here and back in the States, itching to be in on something like this?"

Crenel gave a deep sigh. "Like I said, it's complicated. Nevins has already been caught harboring Mythers on US soil. The problem is, this happened *before* any laws were passed to make it illegal. Since then? No one has seen him."

Penny chewed on her bottom lip. Those laws had only been passed recently in America — and only a couple of months ago in Australia. "So, we not only need to find him, we need to prove that he has creatures that he caught *after* the bans were put in place? How are we going to do that?"

Crenel took a seat and folded his hands in his lap. "There is another option," he told them in an even voice.

Penny leaned back, folded her arms and scowled. "Like what?"

He's too calm, she thought. *Whatever is about to come out of his mouth, I'm going to hate it.*

Crenel's eyes darted toward the sunken spa bath in the corner of his room. While the students had been waiting for Crenel to collect himself, Boots had wriggled straight over to it, flicked the taps on with her tail, and chewed the lid off a travel-sized bottle of bath foam. Now, she frolicked in the frothy water, occasionally sneezing as bubbles got up her nose.

Sensing the attention, the splashing stopped as Boots

lifted her head out of the mountain of froth she had created. She hissed at Agent Crenel.

"No." Penny slammed her hand palm down on the coffee table. "No!"

"We would take every precaution." Crenel raised his hands defensively. "Come on, Penny, you know me. We'd keep her safe, I promise."

Penny shook her head resolutely. "You're *not* using her as bait."

"Agent Crenel, does your wife know about this plan?" Amelia asked haughtily.

"As a matter of fact, yes, she does," Crenel shot back. "And anyway, it's not set in stone." He turned to Penny, his face serious. "You don't have to decide now. There's every chance that we'll get there and find all the evidence we need to arrest this bastard. But if we don't, all I ask is that you keep it in mind."

There was a splash from the corner of the room as Boots flicked herself into a stunning dive and plopped back into the water.

"Let's exhaust all other options first," Penny said. "What else do we know?"

The situation was indeed complex. According to Crenel's sources, Nevins had not only smuggled Mythers from the United States over to Australia, but it was also rumored that he had a number of local creatures as well. Rather than selling them on the black market, however, he'd opened his "sanctuary," a safari experience mostly populated by native Australian animals, with a few magical creatures as the drawcard for wealthy guests.

Penny's stomach clenched, her fury fanned by the idea

of the magnificent creatures born of myth and legend being trapped in cages and paraded like curiosities. "I can't believe he gets away with it."

"The safari expeditions he runs aren't exactly advertised to the public," Crenel told them. "But I have a man who might be able to source us some tickets. It might take me a couple of days to get in touch with him, but he'll come through."

"Wouldn't it be more profitable just to sell the critters?" Red asked. "Keeping them all in one place and letting strangers in to look at them seems risky if they've all been poached."

Crenel shrugged. "He could be relying on the fact that most of the creatures were taken before laws came in preventing it. And he may be using the zoo as a showcase for animals he's actually selling on the side. Who knows, maybe the attraction of magical creatures in a high-end resort experience is worth more than we think."

It only took Agent Crenel a day to get in touch with his source. "There's an event coming up in two days. It's invitation-only, and my friend just happens to have five of them."

"And that gets us?" Penny waited for the punchline.

"That gets us access to the man who can sell us tickets to the magical outback experience at the Flying Crow Eco Resort." Crenel's mouth curled into a snarl as he said the words. Penny knew the very idea of exploiting Mythers disgusted him.

"I take it this is something we'll need to dress up for?" Amelia asked. She darted a triumphant glance at Penny.

"It's the kind of event that will only be attended by billionaires, celebrities, and possibly the Mafia." Crenel looked more uncomfortable about the billionaires than the Mafia. "So yes, I'd say you have to dress up."

"You could have warned us," Penny complained. "The clothes I bought are more suitable for trekking through the bush than going to parties."

"I did warn you!" Crenel shook his head. "I told you to be prepared for anything."

"Anything *in the Aussie outback*," Penny reminded him. "We don't do soirees in the scrub!"

"It's okay," Amelia assured her with a smirk. "*I* came prepared. Not just for me, but for *all* of you." She spread her hands in a wide shrug. "You didn't think all the stuff in those suitcases was for *me*, did you?"

"Yes." Red bore the slap to his midriff rather well. "I've seen your wardrobe, Milly. I know you like to dress nice wherever you go. Why would this be any different?"

Rolling her eyes, Amelia turned to Penny. "Look, I brought a couple of things suitable for a party like this. I even packed a couple of dresses that would fit you—but I didn't have a lot of room. When it comes to it, just remember, beggars can't be choosers."

Penny cringed inwardly, wondering what kind of skimpy, see-through, sequined ensemble Amelia was planning to inflict on her. "What about shoes?"

"I have 'em." Amelia grinned. "Lighten up, Penny. It won't be *that* bad."

CHAPTER THREE

Penny stepped out of the Uber, clutching Cisco's hand for balance as she wobbled on the pair of impossibly high heels Amelia had loaned her.

"I thought you said it wouldn't be this bad?" she pointed out acerbically.

Amelia rolled her eyes. "Don't whine. It doesn't go with the dress."

Penny had to admit, it was a nice dress. The silky emerald-green fabric draped around her neck and hung open almost to her belly button. If not for some strategically placed tape, she wasn't entirely sure how the dress would have stayed on.

"I think you look amazing," Cisco reached back into the car to help Boots out. His suit had been freshly pressed that morning, and his usually messy hair was stylishly slicked back.

Penny fought to keep the color from rising in her cheeks. Although they had spent the last two days together, moving between the hotel pool and bar during the day and sharing a bed at night, his compliments still made her blush. She busied herself with settling Boots on her shoulders, draped like an artistically placed shawl. "Be careful you don't wrinkle the dress, sweetheart," Penny murmured. "And for God's sake, don't dislodge the tape!"

"Oh, shite." Red lifted a polished shoe that dripped gutter water. "Yuck. It's seeping into my socks."

"Red! I can't take you anywhere." Amelia pulled him onto the footpath and slid her arm through his. "Where is the old man? He said he'd meet us here." She looked around, a small frown deepening the crease between her eyebrows. "For that matter, where's the party?"

"Three doors down." Agent Crenel appeared from around a corner, looking, well, *expensive*. The tight curls of his hair appeared to have been freshly trimmed, and instead of worn and aging, the streaks of gray gave him a distinguished look. "And for future reference, I'm not *that* old."

"Well, you'd better be at least old enough to be my dad," Amelia pointed out. "Because that's the cover story we came up with."

Crenel lifted an enquiring eyebrow at Penny. "'Cover story?'"

Penny shrugged. "You know the rule. Always be prepared."

"Whose father am I supposed to be, exactly?" he asked.

"Mine and Penny's," Amelia told him. "Think about it. You're too pale to be Cisco's dad, but you're not pasty enough to be Red's."

"I'm not pasty!" Red protested.

"And the fact that I have one daughter with an American accent like mine and another that sounds like she was raised on an Australian cattle station?" Crenel asked.

Penny yelped. "I'll have you know the nearest cattle station was at least thirty klicks down the road from where I grew up, thank you." She turned to Amelia. "He's got a point, though. You know I can't pull off an American accent, and there's no way either of you could blend in with the locals here."

Crenel looked at Cisco. "Looks like I'm adopting a son."

Cisco shrugged. "It'll pass. Amelia, your tan is about nine shades darker than when we arrived. If anyone asks, we take after our mum."

"As long as I don't have to pretend to be his sister," Amelia said, jabbing a thumb at Red. "That would raise some eyebrows." To illustrate her point, she gave him a kiss.

"Aye, that would be awkward." Red wrapped an arm around Amelia's waist. "So, where are we going? I hope we didn't get this dressed up for nothing."

Penny spun, counting the dark, closed up doorways that lined the backstreet they had been dropped off in. "Three doors down would be that one there," she said. "Number one-seven-one?"

"That's it," Crenel confirmed.

The door in question looked like all the others—peeling paint, grimy edges, and a big fat deadbolt locking it shut.

Crenel approached the door and knocked twice. After a pause, he knocked once more.

"Are you serious?" Cisco muttered.

Penny heard the snick of a lock opening, and a crack of yellow light illuminated the street. Crenel spoke to the person at the door and handed him a brilliant white envelope. The door opened all the way, and a very short man ushered them in.

Penny eyed the bouncer as she walked past him. She almost could have believed he was human. It was the clothes that tipped her off.

"Nice shoes," she commented.

The leprechaun glanced down at his pointy black shoes adorned with big gold buckles, then up at Penny. "Nice snake."

"Thanks."

The leprechaun led the way down a narrow corridor. Penny trailed her fingers over the wall, brushing the painted brick surface.

"Ew, don't do that. It looks dirty," Amelia complained when she noticed. "You know, there are only two kinds of parties a grotty entrance could lead to."

"And what kinds are they?" Penny asked, humoring her.

"We're either going to find a bunch of grotty teenagers snorting cocaine out of ashtrays, or the most luxurious soirée you've ever seen." Amelia patted her hair. "Going by what agent—uhh, *Dad* said, we're heading for the latter."

Their guide ignored them, eventually pushing open another heavy door at the end of the hallway. Music spilled out, a sweet, rhythmic tune from a stringed instrument.

Penny stepped into the room behind Amelia, immediately feeling underdressed for the occasion. All around her, women floated by in expensive cocktail dresses, glittering jewelry draped from their necks, ears, wrists, and fingers. The men had the polished air of millionaires in their immaculate suits and sparkling cufflinks.

"Whoa" Cisco gripped Penny's fingers with sweaty hands. "I was feeling pretty good about myself until I walked in here. Every single person in this place is more beautiful than I am."

Penny turned to him, pulling him close. With a cheeky grin, she kissed his nose. "*Nobody* in this room is more beautiful than you are. Richer, maybe. Nicer car? Almost certainly. But I bet none of them have organized a first date involving Mexican on a rooftop, and a personalized display of water sprites."

"I wouldn't be so sure about that." Cisco's eyes had been searching the room as she spoke, and now rested on the source of the sweet music. "Uhh, what's the story with *that?*"

Penny looked over and blinked. A lady in a blue ball gown sat with her eyes closed in concentration as she strummed the instrument in her hands. It was made of an oversized jawbone. The teeth were strung with fine black fibers that hummed as she plucked them.

Even more surprising than the instrument itself was the audience it drew. A tiny sparrow sat on her left shoulder, and in the crook of one arm, a mousey nose sniffed the air. At her feet sat perhaps the strangest assortment of creatures Penny had ever seen.

Pristine white rabbits sat next to scruffy river rats. A fat pigeon with worn, dirty feathers and a chipped beak nestled beside a perky bluebird. "What the hell?"

The gentle hiss pulled Penny's attention toward Boots, who stared at the musician, mesmerized. Penny tapped Boots' head. The serpent coughed, shook her head, and looked back at Penny.

"That has to be a mythological artifact," Cisco murmured. "Unless Disney princesses have made it across the Veil?"

"I'm pretty sure that if Cinderella and Snow White had popped up, it would be all over the news in an instant." Penny nodded at the musical instrument. "And *that* isn't a princess harp. I wonder what it is."

"That, my dear friends, is a kantele. It belonged to the legendary Väinämöinen." The man who stepped between Penny and Cisco, draping an arm around each of them… wasn't a man. His brilliant green eyes and tightly furled ears took Penny's breath away.

"You're…"

"An elf?" He dipped a low bow. "Santa's favorite helper, at your service."

"You don't work for Santa! You're too…" Red waved a hand at the elf. "*Pretty.*"

The elf just chuckled. "No, I don't. But I find it far less offensive than people thinking I spend all day babysitting hobbits." He stuck a slender hand out. "Tarathriel Inaydar."

"So, what kind of elf are you, then?" Amelia asked. "Other than one who sounds like he was named by one of those computerized name generators."

"The generic sort." Tarathriel winked. "Devastatingly handsome, expert with a bow, and friend to all living creatures."

"So, the rodents came with you?" Red asked, scowling.

Tarathriel nodded. "The kantele isn't from my branch of mythology, though. It attracts my little followers, but the local…well, *rodents* seem to be just as drawn by its music."

He reached for Penny's hand. "As am I, if not as strongly. Would you and your beautiful companion like a dance?"

"I'm fine, thanks." Cisco folded his arms, eyes roaming the room uncomfortably.

Tarathriel smirked. "I was talking about—"

"He knows," Penny interjected. "I'm sorry, I don't dance with strange elves."

Glancing over Tarathriel's shoulder, Penny could see Agent Crenel talking to a thin man with a hooked nose. They were deep in conversation, and Penny didn't expect them to be done any time soon.

Tarathriel followed Penny's gaze. "Your chaperone?" he asked.

Penny shook her head. "He's my boyfriend's father."

Tarathriel lifted a slender eyebrow. "Right. Do you know the man he is talking to?"

Shaking her head a second time, Penny searched for a distraction. Tarathriel's questions were making her uncomfortable, and she didn't want to blow their cover. As if sensing Penny's distress, Boots darted her head against the elf's shoulder.

Tarathriel ducked his head so he could look into Boots' gleaming eyes. "Hello, ancient one." He bowed his head respectfully. "My apologies for not greeting you first."

Boots hissed in return, then heaved herself off of Penny's shoulders into his arms. Coiling her head up, she tapped her nose against his.

Tarathriel grinned. "It is different on this side of the Veil. Before the tearing, those of us born of Myth and Legend kept with our own kind—the Greeks, the Celtic myths, the Indian deities, the new creations. Oh, we crossed paths every now and then, but not like now."

Leaning forward, Tarathriel pressed his forehead against Boots' tiny face.

Unnerved by Boots' immediate affinity to the elf, Penny wasn't sure what to say in response. Thankfully, she was saved.

"Red!" Amelia's outraged hiss was followed by a yelp from her boyfriend as she pinched the soft flesh of his stomach. "This is a refined gathering of individuals, *not* the all-you-can-eat smorgasbord at the local Chinese restaurant."

Red scowled. "You know I don't eat Chinese anymore. That bastard cat won't even let me through the door." He gestured helplessly with hands that clutched at least a dozen tiny pastries. He seemed oblivious to the waiter behind him, scowling over an empty tray.

Heaving a sigh, Red offered the pastries to his friends and their companion. Cisco shook his head with a grimace, and Penny politely refused the slightly squashed hors d'oeuvres.

Tarathriel eyed them. "It seems they have a type of hog meat in them." He shrugged apologetically. "I do not eat animal flesh."

Red muttered something about "vegans" under his breath, then crammed them into his mouth.

Raising her eyes to the ceiling, Amelia gave a frustrated huff. "You didn't offer me any! I'm starving!"

"Sorry!" Red stretched to his full height and ran his eyes over the room, finally spotting another waiter in a far corner. "Look, there's a man over there serving tiny quiches. I'll go get you a dozen."

He disappeared before Amelia could protest.

"Tell your friend not to worry," Tarathriel said softly to Penny. "I have been to quite a number of these gatherings. Those who attend rarely adhere to social conventions."

"We'll fit right in then," Penny murmured. She glanced back at Boots, who had settled quite comfortably into Tarathriel's arms.

"Here comes Crenel—I mean, Dad." Cisco gestured at the agent who was walking toward them purposefully.

"I shall leave you be." Tarathriel unwound Boots from his arms and passed her back to Penny. "I imagine you have important things to discuss with the law enforcement officer pretending to be your father. Farewell!"

Penny groaned while Cisco stared after the elf in awe. "How could he possibly know that?"

"Because you're all *terrible* liars," Amelia told them flatly. "Let's just hope he keeps his mouth shut."

"Look, kids!" Crenel held up a glossy brochure, a forced grin plastered on his face. "I booked a trip!"

"You can drop the charade," Penny said in a low voice. "We've already been outed by the pointy-eared vegan."

Crenel shook his head in despair. "I knew I should have left you back at the hotel. Where's Red?"

"I'm right behind you, Agent Crenel." Red brandished the handful of food he'd plucked off the tray. "Quiche?"

Crenel eyed the food, shrugged, and plucked one from Red's hand. "They're awfully small, aren't they? Fancy party like this, the least they could do is make man-sized portions."

"That's what I told them!" Red exclaimed. He waved his hands as he spoke, scattering crumbs everywhere.

"Settle down, dear," Amelia said. "You're making a mess."

Red looked down and picked some crumbs off his shirt. "Are we done yet? I'd kill for a pizza. A real one, not a teeny little mouse-sized slice topped with rubbish like cashew cheese and caviar."

"Let's make a move." Crenel nodded to the door. "Before one of you creates a scene."

Lightning flashed inside the room as a clap of thunder rang out. Penny clutched her ears, blinking rapidly to clear the bright spots left by the bright light. Around them, people screamed and shoved each other, trying to evacuate the room. "Too late," she yelled at Crenel.

Crenel slumped momentarily. "Just once," he groaned. "Just once, I thought things could go smoothly."

CHAPTER FOUR

Penny eyed the man in the middle of the room. His white beard swung back and forth as he turned his head, brushing against his long red robe.

"Santa?" Red asked timidly.

It wouldn't be the first variation of the myth that had appeared this side of the veil, but Penny had a feeling this man wasn't Kris Kringle.

"I am Väinämöinen!" The man lifted one hand, holding a wooden oar. "It is time. I have returned!" He glowered at the blank stares surrounding him.

Tarathriel whispered in Penny's ear, making her jump. "Really, who buys a magical artifact without knowing who the previous owner was?"

"*That's* the guy who owned the dental harp?" Penny asked in a low voice.

"Kantele," Tarathriel corrected her. "But yes. He lost it eons ago. Made a replacement, I believe, one a bit less…primitive."

"Has he come to get it back?" Penny searched her

memory but was certain this wasn't a myth she had come across in her studies. "Look, Legolas, if you're gonna help out here, I need more information."

Väinämöinen swung toward them. "You!" He jabbed the oar at Tarathriel. "You spoke my name. Have these people forgotten their history?"

Tarathriel stood and cleared his throat. "Mighty wizard, I'm afraid these are not, in fact, the people you served. Those men and women are oceans away and gone for millennia."

Väinämöinen's expression darkened. "Then who is the thief who stole my instrument from its rightful owners?"

"*Stole* it?" a man in a back corner blustered. "I paid half a mil for that damn ukulele."

"Oh, no." Penny shrank back as Väinämöinen seemed to grow taller. A low hum filled the room, undulating like a Gregorian chant. Clouds billowed near the ceiling and threw deep shadows over the room. The hair on Penny's arms stood on end.

"Väinämöinen is a Finnish god, or perhaps just a hero, depending on who you ask." Tarathriel spoke fast, his voice tight with worry. "He has fought gods and monsters, and has unspeakable power."

"Friend or foe?" Cisco snapped. "Can we reason with him?"

Tarathriel shook his head. "I cannot say with certainty. He once served humans, but his legend ceased with the advent of Christianity. It is said he sailed off into the sunset, promising to come back when he was needed. That does not look like a face open to discussion, though."

Väinämöinen's lips parted as his song reached a crescendo. Electric bolts flickered inside the clouds.

"He's singing," Penny said, grabbing Tarathriel's arm. "And he has a magic instrument. Is it music-based magic?"

Tarathriel nodded. "His voice is well known for its god-like quality."

Grinning. Penny snatched out her phone. "Red, Cisco?"

"If you've cooked up some kind of hair-brained, dangerous scheme," Red said, "count me in. Anything is better than this boring party."

"I need one of those speakers." Penny pointed at an expensive sound system in one corner of the room. It was off, but Penny recognized the model. *Saved by the Bluetooth.* "Turn it on and press the button that'll connect it to my phone."

Red and Cisco nodded in unison. They darted across the room as Väinämöinen lifted his arms, his song increasing in tempo.

The kantele lurched out of the hands of the musician and into the air. She snatched at it even as she squealed in terror, but the instrument was already out of her reach. It floated toward the wizard and he snatched it, strumming a discordant note.

The animals rose on their back legs, baring fangs and teeth as they eyed the partygoers.

"Not on my watch," Tarathriel muttered. His eyes glowed green, and he whispered a chant under his breath.

A giant rat skittered into the crowd. Women—and several men—screamed and scattered. A press of bodies flooded to the metal door, crowding against it. A sliver of light shone as it cracked open, only to disappear with a clang as Väinämöinen threw an arm toward it with a high-pitched note.

Penny's breath caught as Red dove behind the sound system. The LED lights of the speaker blinked.

Amelia screamed, *"Rat!"*

Penny looked down and reflexively kicked at the scruffy, snarling rodent headed toward them. Before her foot connected, Tarathriel scooped it up, stroking its head and soothing its frantic rage. As he whispered in its ear, the rat's fur smoothed and the crusted dirt fell away, leaving it clean and happy as it nuzzled the inside of the elf's elbow.

"Defend us, brave soul. Bite his toes and scratch his eyes." Tarathriel set the rat on the floor and it scurried away, quickly lost beneath the long skirts and trampling feet of the frantic people fleeing the wizard's wrath.

Tarathriel gasped. "Oh, dear." He turned to Penny with tortured eyes. "Our fine warrior has failed, thwarted by the violent heel of a fleeing stiletto."

Penny winced. "Ouch. Poor guy."

New Device Available

The notification that popped up on Penny's screen brought a rush of relief. "Let's see if you can out-sing this, you hairy bastard." She selected the speaker, set the volume to max, and pressed play.

The dulcet tones of Freddy Mercury cut Väinämöinen's song short as the first line of *Don't Stop Me Now* split the air. Above the speaker, the storm clouds retreated.

Väinämöinen gaped, then gave a long, loud, musical yell. The speaker exploded.

"There goes that plan," Penny yelled over the operatic wailing.

Her idea, however, hadn't entirely failed. From the other side of the room, Penny could hear snatches of the song.

"Is that…is Red *singing*?" Amelia asked.

The song's chorus erupted, a little off-key and not quite in time, but loudly enough that Penny could clearly pick out Cisco's voice alongside Red's. With a smirk, Penny sucked in a breath. On the next line, she joined them. She sang as loud as she could, throwing herself into it while she played air guitar.

When a rich baritone added to the mix, Penny almost fell over. Agent Crenel gave her a sly wink as he continued, while Amelia implored the people nearby to add their voices.

It was working. The cloud roiled, parted, roiled again. The flashes of light had ceased, and the animals enlisted into Väinämöinen's strange army sat on their haunches, blinking in confusion as the wizard's magic failed to penetrate the rock song.

Väinämöinen gave a yell of frustration. With one loud, melodious call, he vanished in a flash of bright light, leaving behind nothing but a wisp of smoke.

The impromptu rock rendition fell away and silence filled the room.

It broke when someone hooted with exuberant joy, "How great was that?" Cheers of approval went up as people began to congratulate the host for throwing such an exciting party.

Tarathriel gave a long-suffering sigh. "I did warn you. These events rarely follow the usual social conventions."

"Are they… Was all of that…" Shaking her head, Amelia

gave up trying to make sense of the situation. When a waitress passed with a tray of champagne, she scooped up two glasses and held one out to Penny, downing hers in a single gulp. "If you can't beat 'em, join 'em, right?"

"Wrong." Crenel raised an arm and gestured for Cisco and Red to follow them. "We're leaving. Now. I don't want to be here when Gandalf reappears."

"Why, Agent Crenel," Penny said as she hooked her arm through his. "Did I just hear you make a pertinent pop culture reference?"

Crenel scowled and plucked the glass from her free hand. "No drinking on the job." Despite his words, he gulped down the stolen drink. "Now, take pity on an old man. I just want to make it back to the hotel without any more trouble, okay?"

Amelia slapped a textbook down on the tiny hotel coffee table. "Trust Crenel to take this fake dad thing way too far."

"Tell me about it," Penny grumbled. "I mean, I get that you're missing out on a holiday and all, but I haven't been home for a year, and now that I am? I'm stuck in this crappy hotel."

Amelia winced as she looked around the opulent hotel room. She glanced pointedly at the thick carpet, the expensive sheets, and the gigantic flatscreen TV hanging on the wall. "It's not *that* crappy," she said. "And although I hate to admit it, he does have a point. Dean March isn't going to give us a free pass on any of our exams." She flipped the textbook open, rifling through pages until she found the spot she wanted. She pressed her left index finger on a line of text, then looked at Penny beseechingly.

Penny threw her hands up in defeat and stomped over to her suitcase. She pulled out a rainbow pencil case and a matching notebook and tossed them to Amelia, who caught them one-handed. "You're lucky I brought the stationery shop with us," Penny told her.

Amelia flashed a winning grin. "Lucky and incredibly grateful."

Penny dragged out a thick notebook of her own and set to reading notes for the upcoming exams. The semester would end in two short weeks, and their flights weren't booked for three. Thankfully— or not, Penny thought with a silent snort—Dean March had organized for the relevant exams to be available online. Agent Crenel would supervise the students as they completed them to ensure the Academy's high standards were kept throughout the unorthodox process.

Optimal salt to water ratio for aerosol application is one part salt to sixteen parts water, Penny read. She paused and screwed up her face, trying to remember if the figures she had jotted down were by weight or volume. Unable to remember, she wrote a note in the margins to double-check later. She read on, reciting the facts and statistics in a silent whisper, doing her best to commit them to memory.

Ding!

Penny bit down on her momentary frustration and glanced at her phone. She quickly read Cisco's message before it went back to sleep.

The old man just left. Wanna sneak out?

She tapped a quick reply.

Studying. Hey, do you remember if the one:sixteen saltwater aerosol ratio is by weight or volume?

Oh my God, Penny. When did you get old and boring?

Penny scowled at his response but grinned when a second message quickly followed it.

It's by weight. I know this because I made a deck of flashcards. Do you want me to duck over so we can practice together?

Colour me impressed, Penny wrote back. **Sure.**

In the end, Penny went to Cisco. They quizzed each other ruthlessly, not stopping until Penny groaned and flopped onto the plush carpet. "I can't do this anymore. I'm so bored."

"Let's spice it up," Cisco suggested. "Drinking game. You get a question wrong, you down a shot."

"Let's do it." Penny rolled to her feet and went over to raid the minibar.

Cisco stopped her. "There's no way we can afford to get drunk on hotel booze. Check my suitcase—there's a farewell gift from Paddy tucked in the side."

Penny did as she was asked, digging through the rumpled stack of clothing in Cisco's bag to find the whiskey. She found it wrapped in a pair of jeans.

"First of all, who taught you to pack like that?" she asked. "And second, jeans? It's a thousand degrees out there. You'll melt if you wear those."

Cisco shrugged. "I'll be fine. Mom and Dad used to travel a ton. Never to Australia, but to places that get just as hot."

"You're a practiced traveler, and you still pack like a five-year-old running away from home for the first time?" Penny asked with a chuckle. She found two shot glasses in the hotel cabinet and brought them over.

Cisco took the glasses and whiskey and poured two

shots. "It's a guy thing. Now, what are the three critical hit points on a vampire?"

It was two whole days until Agent Crenel let them out again.

"And what do you do if you see a Myther?" he asked Penny for the third time.

Rolling her eyes, she answered. "Report it, ignore it, or —"

"There is no 'or!'" Crenel snapped. "If you're going to be a smartass, you can all stay home."

"We're tourists, remember? All I was going to say is that we can ignore it, report it, or snap a cute picture of it like any other tourist would do." Penny plucked her room key out of Crenel's hand. He had been holding it hostage but seemed to have forgotten that as his frustration with her flippancy rose.

He threw his hands up in defeat. "You know what? Get yourself killed. I don't care! I'll only be sacrificing my career, my marriage, and—"

It was Penny's turn to cut the special agent off. "Come on—as if Dean March thinks you have any chance of reining us in." Penny patted him on the shoulder consolingly. "She knows we're a bunch of incorrigible young adults who think we know better, and that we all have a problem with authority and immortality complexes. She won't blame you in the *slightest*." Penny dropped the key into her purse, then zipped it closed and slung it over her shoulder.

Agent Crenel eyed her. "Sometimes I wonder if you've ever actually met my wife."

"I have. And I've met you. If she didn't kill you over the Kraken incident, she's not going to." Penny slipped on a pair of sandals at the door. "Make sure you hang the Do Not Disturb sign on the door when you leave. See you later, Boots."

Boots hissed angrily, clearly upset at the agent's insistence that the Myther stay behind.

The door clicked shut behind her just before Crenel's muffled yell came. "I hate you, Penny Hingston. You know that, right?"

"I love you too, Agent Crenel!" she replied cheerily as she headed away from the room with a skip in her step.

"Do I need to be worried?" Cisco was waiting in the corridor with Red and Amelia beside him. "I never pegged you for someone who liked older men, but..."

"Can you believe he's still giving us a hard time about going out?" Penny groaned. "That whole thing with what's-his-name and his tooth-guitar wasn't even our fault!"

"If we were in a five hundred mile radius of any kind of trouble, it was our fault." Amelia shook her head. "You know how he thinks."

"I know if our asses are still hanging around when he comes out of that room, he's going to give us another lecture. Let's get out of here." Penny led the way to the hotel's elevators and pressed the button that would take them down. They crammed inside, Red squeezing himself into a corner to make room for the elderly couple already inside.

"Morning!" the man said.

"G'day!" Red tipped an imaginary Akubra to complement his horrible attempt at an Australian accent.

"Oh, Americans!" the woman immediately gushed.

Red gave her a quizzical look. "Irish, actually. What, was my Aussie no good?"

The old woman laughed. "Nobody actually says that here, dear. Anyone who does is a tourist—and *usually* one from America."

"I guess I've been rubbing off on him," Amelia confessed. She held a hand out. "I'm Amelia, and that big lug is Red. That handsome guy there is Cisco, and this is Penny." She cupped a hand and whispered loudly, "She's local."

"I'm Ella." The woman smiled and gestured at her husband. "This is Ross. Are you from Sydney, dear?" she asked Penny.

Penny shook her head. "I'm from Larrabee. It's about three hours north-west of the city."

Ella smiled again. "How lovely. Ross, that's a lovely area, isn't it?"

Ross shrugged. "Apart from the heat, sure."

Penny grinned. "That pretty much sums up the whole country, you know."

"Not for us," Ross assured her. "We've got a little chalet up at Cradle Mountain. It's a lovely place down there, even if everyone forgets Tasmania is part of Australia."

The elevator dinged, and the couple shuffled out toward the lobby as they wished Penny and her friends all the best. The doors slid closed again.

"Everyone in Australia is so nice," Cisco said. "Well, apart from some of the jerks at that party."

"Cisco, those jerks at the party and that little old lady and man are the only people you've met in the country so far." Another ding and Penny stepped out of the elevator into the suffocating humidity of the underground parking garage. "Trust me, there are plenty of assholes around here. Some awesome people, sure, but also assholes."

They piled into the small car, both men quiet until Penny nosed the vehicle into the busy street. "So, uhh, Penny?" Cisco cleared his throat. "Red and I were thinking…"

"That shopping sucks, and you don't want to come. Right?" Amelia twisted around to glare at the two boys from the passenger seat. "You could have told us that *before* we left."

"That wasn't what I was going to say," Cisco protested.

"It wasn't?" Red asked. "That's what you were rehearsing earlier."

Groaning in defeat, Cisco faced Amelia. "We were just thinking, you know, we might find somewhere to sit and have a drink. Or something. While you *shop*." He said the last word with distaste as if he was describing something he had picked off his shoe.

Amelia laughed. "Fine with us, right, Penny?"

Penny nodded. "Sure. To be honest, we didn't want you there anyway. It sucks taking guys shopping. You rush past all the good stuff and make stupid jokes when you see the lingerie section."

"Why were you going to make us come, then?" Cisco asked.

"We felt sorry for you!" Penny said. "Look, there are a couple of trendy pubs right around the corner from where

I'm taking Amelia. Just up from there is a tenpin bowling place. You can spend the morning there, we'll do our shopping, and then we'll catch up for lunch and head to the zoo, okay?"

Both boys brightened at the sound of that. "Really? You'll let us go?" Red asked.

"*Let* you go? Babe, we're not prison guards. You can go wherever you want… As long as it suits us. Which it does." Amelia winked at her boyfriend.

"And we are so grateful to our overlords," Red snorted.

Amelia sighed. "If I could reach you…"

"You'd kiss me cheek and call me beautiful?" Red guessed.

"Not exactly."

Penny grinned at her friends' banter as she drove. The outing had already put her in the best mood she had felt since arriving in the scorching heat. *Speaking of the heat…* "Hey, Amelia, can you pass me my water, please? It's on the floor by your feet."

"Sure." Amelia bumped around, reaching under her seat. "Here it is. Do you want me to— Uh, Penny?"

Penny glanced at her friend briefly before her eyes shifted to the bottle. Startled, she wrenched her gaze back to the road. "Jesus. Yes, open it, so she can hear me curse her out."

Amelia unscrewed the lid and Boots slithered out of the bottle, dripping water onto Amelia's lap. She hissed gently and hung her head in remorse.

"You know *I'm* the one that's going to get in trouble for this, right?" Penny demanded. Boots nodded morosely.

Penny let out a groan of exasperation. "You poor thing. You were feeling just as cooped up as we were, huh?"

Boots nodded again, this time eagerly. Sensing she had already been forgiven, the serpent lifted up to butt Penny's cheek.

"All right. "Penny pushed her away, not wanting her concentration diverted from the road. "On one condition. *You* get to babysit the boys."

CHAPTER SIX

To Penny, it felt like hardly any time at all had passed when they next met back up with Cisco, Red, and Boots. Red's cheeks were tinged with pink, and Cisco's grin held just a hint of drunken sloppiness. Even Boots was a little wobbly.

"We leave you three unattended for what, an hour?" Penny asked. "And you get drunk?"

Cisco held up a finger. "First of all, we're not drunk." He straightened a second finger. "And B, you were gone for four hours. *Four hours*! What the hell kind of shopping takes four hours?"

Penny opened her mouth to protest as she flicked a glance at her watch. She snapped her mouth shut when she saw he was right.

Clinging to Cisco's shoulders, Boots chuckled.

"Shut up, you," Penny grumbled.

"We're girls, Cisco." Amelia shoved her three full bags at him. "It's not as easy as walking into a shop, picking up nine identical shirts, and shoving them at the cashier."

Cisco glanced at Red for support, but his friend just shrugged. "You have to admit, Cisco, they do dress better than us."

"Fine. But we're not drunk." Cisco adjusted his grip on Amelia's bags and held a hand out to take Penny's. She refused, immediately regretting it when he passed his burden over to Red and raised his empty hands. "We've eaten, we've drunk. Drank. Not drunk, remember? Where to next?"

"Let's drop our bags at the car first," Penny said. "It's only a five-minute walk to the ferry, which will take us straight to the zoo."

Amelia grinned in delight. "I want to see the tiny pandas. Do you have any idea how cute they are?"

"I want to cuddle a drop bear," Red stated. "Not the bitey ones, the cuddly ones."

"That would be a koala," Penny corrected him. "Drop bears aren't even real. At least, they weren't before the veil tore."

"Aye, those ones."

They soon had Penny's and Amelia's haul packed away safely. They arrived just in time to grab the ferry across Sydney Harbor, a trip enjoyed by all but Red, who sat by the railing looking more than a little green around the gills. Boots spent the trip frolicking in the water, only somersaulting back onto the deck of the ferry when it docked on the other side. The handful of passengers who had been watching her clapped.

The recent data had shown that more humans were gaining the ability to see Mythers every day, but this was the first time Penny had seen that change. Boots flicked her head, sprinkling water on the ferry's deck, and slithered over to Penny.

"Nuh-uh." Penny wagged a finger at the serpent. "You're not getting in my bag all wet."

Boots shook again, sending a shower of water into the air. The spray caught the sunlight, scattering into a brilliant rainbow for a moment before falling away. The snake and the deck around her were dry.

Penny held the bag open for Boots to climb in, but couldn't resist rolling her eyes. "Show-off."

From the dock, they were ushered toward a cable car. Penny jumped in without hesitation, grinning excitedly to Cisco, who quickly joined her.

Red eyed the car that left before them, wincing when it began to swing gently in the stiff afternoon breeze. "Boats *and* heights? Do ye hate me?"

Amelia glared at him. "If you throw up on me, so help me I'll—"

Red turned big, sick puppy dog eyes her way. "Pat me head and rub me poorly tum-tum?"

Unable to argue with such a pathetic display, Amelia just sighed. She didn't complain when his grip on her knee tightened as the cable car jerked, then began crawling up the hill. Instead, she patted his hand and did her best to distract him—or possibly bore him—by giving him a detailed rundown of everything she and Penny had purchased earlier. Despite the occasional jolting halt as the cars ahead reached their destination, Amelia kept on talking.

"But I told the shop assistant that green just isn't my

color, you know? Emerald, maybe, or forest. But not *green*! I mean, do I *look* like I—"

The crackle of an intercom cut off her diatribe about the various shoe colors she had looked at.

"*Attention, passengers. Due to a small problem at the zoo entrance, we'll be bringing everyone back to the bottom. Don't worry, you'll get a full refund if we're not up and running in under thirty minutes.*"

"What?" Amelia snapped. "We're almost to the top. Why would they drag us back down?"

Penny pressed her face against the window to try to see what was going on ahead. The car swung as it lurched to a halt, allowing her a quick glimpse of the platform ahead.

The small creature that launched itself toward the car in front of her looked familiar but not. It slipped off the safety glass, caught itself on one of the cables underneath, and lazily swung back onto the grass below.

She leaned over and pressed the silver button under the intercom, hoping it would allow her to communicate with the operator. "Is someone there? I'm in the next car due to land. You need to take us up there and drop us off."

"What the hell is going on, Penny?" Red moaned.

Penny grinned. "It looks like you're going to get to cuddle that drop bear sooner than expected."

"*Car twenty-seven, that's not gonna happen. There is a, um, situation. It's not safe for tourists.*"

Penny depressed the button again. "We're not tourists. We work with the FBI, and this is exactly the sort of situation we are trained to handle. I can see you have security guards up there, but I can also see they're struggling to deal with the threat while keeping the visitors safe. Please. Let us help."

"Penny, they're not just going to take us up there." Cisco gave an apologetic shrug. "They don't know us from a bar of soap. They can't just —"

The cable car lurched forward as a new announcement came over the speaker.

"Apologies, ladies and gentlemen. We have one last car to drop-off before I bring you back to safety. Don't panic, just sit tight. We'll have you down in no time."

"They can and they will." Penny snatched up her handbag from the seat beside her. "In fact, I don't think they have a choice. Amelia, did you bring an emergency kit with you?"

Amelia nodded, and after a moment of digging, pulled out the small black bag marked with the Academy insignia. "I'm glad I stocked this thing before we left."

"What the hell have you *got* in there?" Penny asked as a handful of small plastic vials clattered to the ground.

"They wouldn't let us bring guns," Amelia said. "But they didn't say anything about spray bottles." She scooped up the vials and named each one as she slotted it back into its place in her kit. Apart from the standard holy water and salty water, Amelia had procured wolfsbane and mandrake extracts, dispersed silver, and a single dose of a love potion. She screwed up her face as she named the last one and took extra care in securing it.

Red cocked an eyebrow. "Love potion?"

Amelia grimaced. "If someone's drink gets spiked, a second dose will act as an antidote."

"None of that is going to help us fight those." Cisco

pointed out the window, where the landing platform rapidly approached. A cluster of small fluffy animals awaited them.

Penny pursed her lips, examining them. They really did look like koalas. Well, meth-addict koalas after a three-day bender. The small beasts had patchy fur, and the normally soft tufts of hair covering their ears were matted and spiked. Under large leathery noses, the animals bared pointed fangs, snarling and blinking their glowing red eyes.

"Fascinating," Penny said.

"You mean 'terrifying,'" Cisco corrected her. "And I noticed that no one answered my question."

"You didn't ask one," Penny pointed out. "But I'm in a good mood, so I'll humor you. I have two pairs of knuckle dusters, three small stakes, and a sling. Amelia, do you have any spring-loaded nets? I have two."

"Just the one," Amelia said. "But those guys are teeny-tiny. I bet I can get at least three of them in one try."

Red piped up. Strangely, the new threat they faced had brought the color back to his cheeks, and he no longer seemed nervous about their journey in the cable car. "I have a telescopic baton in my pocket."

Amelia pouted. "I thought you were just happy to see me."

"I'm always happy to see you," Red said with a grin. "I keep the baton in my back pocket."

"I've suddenly realized I'd rather spend my afternoon with the drop bears," Cisco groaned. "Can I take the sling? I've been practicing with one ever since there was a rumor that a giant Cyclops was seen north of Portland."

Penny handed Cisco the sling and a bag of custom-made stones, hard and dense for maximum damage. She armed herself with the stakes and a knuckle duster. Red had taken a small crossbow from Amelia's bag, and Amelia clutched a plastic spray bottle.

She caught Penny's skeptical glance. "Look, Australia does scare me a little bit. I did some research on the snakes, the spiders, the Bunyips, the giant man-eating crocodiles, those birds that peck you in the head, and drop bears, and it turns out, some people think drop bears are just rabid koalas." She lifted an empty vial labeled red mercury. "If they're rabid, they can be cured, and if they can be cured, *this* little number will do it. That's my theory, anyway. If I'm wrong, you'll have to watch my back while I figure something else out."

Penny nodded appreciatively. "Wow. I spent a whole semester studying Australian myths, and I'm pretty sure you know more than I do."

"Not your fault you had a shit teacher," Cisco grumbled.

Penny shrugged, then stood as their ride lurched to a halt. "I know. I just have to resign myself to the fact that nobody knows more about rainbow serpents than I do." She looked down at the subject of her statement. "What do you say, love? Are we ready?"

Boots chuckled and ducked her head in a nod.

Penny grinned down at her. "Let's do this."

CHAPTER SEVEN

The door to the cable car rattled opened and a very worried face popped in. "Danny said you guys are here to help. Do you really know how to take care of situations like this?"

Penny jerked her head in a brisk nod. " It's your lucky day. We work with the FBI in the States. Anyone hurt?"

The white-faced man winced. "Yeah. They tore into a French lady who was trying to protect her kid. And Jamie, from Tickets? I mean, she's still alive, but…"

"What's your name?" Amelia asked kindly.

"Terry. Terry O'Neill. I run the— Holy shit! Holy shit, don't move! There's a… There's a snake in your car!" To his credit, he didn't run, as much as it looked like he wanted to.

Penny moved so that her face obscured his view of Boots. She waited for a moment until his eyes focused on her. "It's okay, the snake is with us. She's my friend."

Before Terry could focus his terror on the serpent behind them again, Cisco jumped in. "What about your security, Terry? What's their protocol for a situation like this?"

Terry shrugged. "I dunno, man. I just work the cars. I've only been here a month!"

"We need cages," Penny said. "We'll do our best to catch the little bastards, but we need somewhere to put them when we do."

Terry shook his head, eyes wide. "I told you, I just do the cars. I don't have any cages!"

Gritting her teeth and trying to stay patient, Penny patted his shoulder. "I know you don't. But you can communicate with people, right? That's how you knew we were here to help."

Understanding dawned, and Terry nodded eagerly. "I'll get on the radio right now." He darted back into the tiny kiosk next to the cable car landing, and Penny heard the snap of a lock immediately after.

"Coward," Red muttered.

Amelia elbowed him in the gut. "He's just a kid. Well, our age, but still. He's not trained for this."

Penny grinned. "But we are. You guys ready to have some fun?"

Penny edged forward, her knees bent and her eyes locked on her target. She was vaguely aware of the line of security guards holding back tourists, who, rather than being sensibly afraid of the sharp-toothed, red-eyed little monsters, seemed to be preoccupied with trying to take selfies and get closer for a better shot.

"Idiots," Penny muttered. She spared a glance at Boots, who was to her left. "I bet they'll pay attention to you, dear. Can I put you on security detail?"

Boots ducked ahead again and slithered toward the cluster of people. Even before she got there, several of the people started to draw back, disconcerted by the sight of a snake heading toward them. Penny knew that Boots' watchful eye would not only prevent any of the drop bears from getting near the tourists, but her presence would also help toward scaring the tourists away from the clusterfuck before her.

"It *had* to be in a zoo," Cisco muttered behind her. "There are people everywhere. We need to get this under control and fast."

Penny gave a quick nod, eyeing a single drop bear that had climbed out of the writhing nest of mammals and taken a few steps toward them. She kept her stance low and slowly edged toward it. "Come on, little buddy."

There was a movement in the crowd, and Penny darted a glance over just in time to see three large metal cages being passed down the line of security guards.

Penny reached into her back pocket and withdrew one of her nets and a small stake. The situation wasn't ideal. With three nets for perhaps a dozen targets, they would have to take out at least some of the drop bears directly. However, the one headed toward her had clearly separated itself from the group and would be an easy catch.

Penny lifted her arm, ready to throw the spring-loaded net.

The drop bear pounced. It launched itself directly at

her, shooting through the air and covering the impossible distance in the blink of an eye.

Only Penny's reflexes saved her. She shoved a hand forward, jamming the tiny portable stake in the beast's mouth. The drop bear twisted to the ground, shaking its head in confusion and fury as it tried to dislodge the item wedging its mouth wide open.

"I guess that's one way to incapacitate a mouthful of pointy fangs," Penny muttered. She waited for the Myther to give one more violent shake of its head, then punted it across the small clearing with a well-placed boot. The drop bear sailed through the air like a wriggling football, crashing to the ground a short distance from Boots.

"Someone needs to teach you to play soccer," Red scolded. He held a drop bear aloft by the scruff of its neck as it twisted in his grip, trying frantically to bite him. "That was a terrible kick." Red gave the bear a solid punch, then tossed the dazed animal toward Amelia.

"Is the mercury working?" Penny yelled. Amelia's answer was drowned out by feral screeching as another drop bear launched itself at Penny. This time she met the creature mid-air with the sole of her boot. It tumbled to the ground, shook its head, and pounced at her again. Penny slammed an arm against its jaw, narrowly avoiding the animal's vicious teeth. "I didn't hear you, come again?" She grabbed the drop bear by the scruff of its neck as Red had and looked up at Amelia.

"I said, it looks like it's working!" Amelia held up two thumbs to reinforce her words. To Penny's shock, one of the drop bears was nestled on her shoulder, placidly chewing her hair.

"Damn, you're officially more of a card-carrying Aussie than I am." Penny dangled her fluffy attacker from one hand, then whirled it like a discus. It sailed through the air toward Amelia, who already had the spray bottle aimed toward it.

"Take that, you hairy bastard!" Amelia squirted the creature in the face, then caught it, throwing it back over her head to where Red was waiting. He clutched it by the scruff, letting it scrabble and claw the air until it settled.

As the animal stilled, its eyes faded to a soft brown, and when it shook, coarse fur sprinkled the ground, leaving a soft, luxurious coat instead.

"Magic!" Penny ducked as another drop bear flew over her head. A glance back let her see Cisco lunge for it, and Penny turned her attention to the remaining Mythers.

They had spread out now and were eyeing the newcomers warily.

Three darted forward, scurrying at Penny in a coordinated attack. She dropped into a defensive stance, kicked the first one, and whirled to meet the second.

She blocked with a knee, punched down, jabbed the third with an elbow, then planted a boot in its ass. A downward chop sent the first bear face-first into the ground, and a second kick punted it Boots' way. The serpent flicked her tail and caught it, then happily curled around it, trapping the drop bear in her scaly rainbow coils.

Punch, jab, knee, chop, kick. Penny fought smoothly, avoiding teeth and claws except for a few minor scratches. Three bears became two, then four, then three, then two again.

A loud rip made her wince. She responded with a snap

kick that sent a drop bear sailing. It landed with a crunch and didn't get up.

Penny glared at her last opponent. "You wanna bite me, fine. But if you tear my jeans again, you'll end up like your buddy over there."

The drop bear's red eyes flickered, then faded to brown. Penny straightened, confused until it turned and she saw a circle of glistening droplets on the back of its head.

Behind it, Amelia winked.

"All done?" Penny glanced around, panting. The metal cages now held bright-eyed koalas, while the cluster of rabid drop bears tangled in one of the nets slowly stilled. One by one, they blinked confused brown eyes at the watching tourists. Boots had a koala nestled in a loose nest of coiled muscle. She nuzzled its head and booped her nose on the koala's.

"All done." Amelia flipped the bottle into her other hand and reached up to high-five Penny. The clap of their hands was followed by more—a slow clap from one of the watching tourists was quickly drowned out by loud applause.

The momentary elation of being lauded by a bunch of zoo visitors was quickly dampened by the reality of what had happened. Penny sighed, then turned her head away from the sea of cellphones pointed at them.

"We're gonna be in so. Much. Trouble." She motioned for the cable car operator. "Hey, buddy. I left my handbag in the car. Do you have it?"

He nodded. "Yeah, but it's down bottom. I'll get Danny to send it up."

Resolutely ignoring the hoots and cheers behind them, Penny jerked a nod. "Thanks."

She stared down the cable, watching as the dangling cars kicked back to life. The first one to arrive was empty of passengers. Terry darted forward to unlatch the door and slide it open to reveal Penny's handbag sitting on a seat…right beside a carton of beer.

Terry blushed. "The beer's for you. To say thanks. From Danny and me, I mean. I thought I was gonna get eaten! And…" He paused, bashful. "Could we maybe have an autograph?"

Penny stared at him for a minute. Then she burst out laughing.

CHAPTER EIGHT

They decided to stay at the zoo after Penny pointed out that returning early would only maximize the hours Crenel had available to lecture them about laying low and staying out of trouble.

They meandered past the animals, paying equal attention to lions and giraffes as to the dripping ice creams in their hands.

"Penny, when do we get to meet Bindi?" Red blurted at one point.

"Bindi?" Amelia slapped his shoulder. "You came here to meet *a girl*?"

"I'm a fan, that's all!" he protested.

Penny shook her head, chuckling. "Wrong zoo, Red. Bindi's is up north."

He sighed. "At least it'd be cooler up there."

Cisco stopped. "Do you even know how globes work? We're south of the equator. Going up means it gets hotter, you moron."

"Look, my brain is fried from the heat, okay?" Red

shoved the last half of his soggy cone in his mouth. "It's hot, and I don't like it. I'm pretty sure Frodo didn't sweat this much in Mordor."

"That's because he's not a whiny baby," Amelia said, leading him away. "Come on. There's a kiosk selling frozen Coke over there."

"Do you ever look at those two and wonder how they make it work?" Penny mused quietly.

"Every damn day." Cisco shot her a quick grin. "But they do."

Penny's back pocket vibrated, and she pulled her phone out. A message flashed on the screen. "Speaking of things that never change…"

"Agent Crenel?" Cisco asked.

"Yeah. He wants to know, and I quote, 'What the hell were you thinking?'"

Cisco chuckled. "At least he didn't insinuate we *don't* think."

The phone buzzed again and Penny snorted. "You spoke too soon."

"Man, he's going to put us on house arrest. Or hotel arrest. Is that a thing?" Cisco rubbed a hand through his hair, clearly unhappy with the prospect of spending more days cooped up in the hotel.

"Well, I know one place he might let us escape to." Penny stared at her phone, a smile touching her lips. "Somewhere we can't get into any trouble. At least, any trouble that'll go viral online."

"Where's that?" Cisco looked dubious. "Crenel isn't gonna buy it. There's nowhere on Earth that will keep us out of trouble."

"Geez, Cisco, you sound like you agree with him," Penny teased.

———

"Sure, you can go." Agent Crenel poured himself another scotch from the minibar.

Penny watched, frowning. "What?"

"You can go." Crenel downed the scotch and poured a third. He didn't drink that one right away, instead taking a seat in one of the plush armchairs by the window of his room. "Look, I give up. I officially, completely, unequivocally quit trying to keep you people out of trouble."

"Really?" Amelia walked over and placed the back of her hand on the agent's forehead. "Are you okay?"

Crenel brushed her hand away, irritated. "I'm fine."

Penny's eyes narrowed. "What aren't you telling us?" She knew he wouldn't let them out of his sight unless… "Wait. You've heard from your home office, haven't you?"

Her only answer was a scowl.

Red tipped his head quizzically. "What does that mean?"

Penny watched the agent's face continue to drop. "It *means*," she crowed, "that they saw the videos of us taking care of the situation at the zoo. And they *liked* it!"

Crenel huffed and tossed his drink back. "Do you have to rub it in?"

"Ha!" Penny's fist punched the air. "Let me guess, they told you to let us clean up any messes we want. Instead of laying low and avoiding trouble, they *want* us to go out and find it."

"It's terrible advice!" Agent Crenel snapped. "The more

eyes we draw down here, the harder our mission will be. What if the wrong person has seen those videos? Our poacher will go into hiding, and all those kidnapped Mythers will be smuggled away before we have a chance to find them."

Penny gave a long-suffering sigh. "You *know* we didn't go out intentionally looking for trouble."

Crenel held on to his scowl for a moment longer, but eventually, his face softened. "I know. And I know that if I had been there, I probably would have done exactly the same thing you did. Well…" This time his look of annoyance seemed directed inwards. "I probably would have shot the feral little bastards. You did a better job than I could have. But that doesn't mean I have to like the attention!"

"Well, where we're going, there won't *be* any attention." Penny gave him a reassuring smile. "I mean, Larrabee is in the middle of nowhere. It has a population of about a dozen people. There's stuff-all internet reception, and half the people who live there wouldn't even know how to use a smartphone."

"Which is why I'm letting you go." Crenel spread his hands in defeat. "It's that or continue letting you run around a city with a population of five million, full of tourists, and full of the Mythers that came with them."

Penny leaned down to give the agent a quick hug, ignoring the uncomfortable look on his face. "Thanks for not grounding us, fake-dad." She stood, catching Amelia's mournful look. "What's wrong? Don't you want to come check out my hometown?"

Amelia lifted mournful eyes to Penny's. "What am I going to *wear*?"

The rental car zipped down the long country road, the only vehicle in sight. It had probably been twenty minutes since they had last seen another car—a once-white Land Rover covered in dried mud whose driver had been friendly enough to give them a quick wave as they passed.

"Are we nearly there?" Amelia asked, not for the first time.

Penny nodded at a distant billboard reading, Fruit and Toot, 5 km. The paint was faded but not so much so that the words on it had disappeared. "Yup."

A few minutes later, Penny pulled off the road in front of a weathered hotel. Amelia squinted out the window. "Do we need to stop for gas?"

"We'll need to get some before we leave," Penny confirmed. "But we stopped because we're here."

Amelia pushed open her car door and stepped out into the low gutter. She rested both hands on her hips, looking first to the left, then to the right. "Where's *here*? Penny, this isn't a town. This is four shops, a rundown hotel, and a shelter by the train tracks."

"Yup. That's my home." Penny strode up the hotel steps and crossed the wide veranda. "Hello? Gaz, are you in?"

Shuffling footsteps preceded the elderly, overweight man who shambled into the bar area of the hotel. "Penny? Hey, didn't expect to see you here today. Where have you been lately?"

"I went missing for a year and a half, and you only just noticed?" Penny laughed. "America, Gaz. I've been in America. I'm only back in town for a couple of days, though. I know I didn't call ahead, but can you spare a couple of rooms?"

Slapping a dirty rag on the counter, Gaz shook his head. "I'd give you a room if you were some asshole townie, but I like you too much. We've been overrun by cockies. Not so bad that you'd notice in the daylight, but unless you want the bastards crawling on your face while you sleep, you don't want to stay here."

Penny shuddered. "That's disgusting."

Gaz shrugged. "It is what it is. I've got an exterminator coming out, but he won't be here until tomorrow. Until then, no food and closed bottles only. Dave's beer is cheaper anyway. You know that." He brightened as an idea came to him. "Hey, maybe he can put you up for the night. It won't be flash, but it's better than sleeping in your car, right?"

"Bloody good idea, Gaz." Penny grinned. "Damn shame the kitchen's closed, though. Your maggot bags are the best in the world."

She waved farewell and headed to the bottle shop next door, her friends trailing behind her. As the screen door of the ancient hotel banged shut behind them, Cisco grabbed Penny's arm.

"Was that some kind of secret code?" he asked. "What's a cocky? And maggots? Tell me you don't eat maggots."

Penny stared at him in disbelief for a moment. Then, she burst out laughing. "Oh my... You..." She couldn't get a coherent sentence past the giggles.

"A cocky is a roach," Amelia said carefully. "I know that much, only because we had one in our dorm room, and it took me about five minutes to decipher what she was screaming about while stomping on the bed."

"And the maggots?" Cisco asked.

Red was already chuckling. "It's a pie," he explained. "Which is more like a pasty, really. Not like those bloody things they serve back at the Academy. That horrible pumpkin concoction nearly made me sick."

Amelia nudged him with an elbow. "Didn't stop you from eating two in one sitting."

"Aye. But it still doesn't hold up to a chunky beef filling, dripping with gravy and full of tasty veg." Red rubbed his tummy. "Is there somewhere else we can get a pie? I'm starving!"

Finally able to control her breathing enough to speak, Penny said, "You've already made a stop for snacks once. How are you still hungry?"

"I'm a growin' boy!" he protested. "I wouldn't be me if I didn't have an appetite."

"Fair enough. Let's sort out our accommodation for tonight, then we can go grab some Chinese food." Penny ducked inside the bottle shop, smiling at the familiar jingle of the bell on the door. "It's no maggot bag, but I know how bad you've been pining for some good fried rice since you got kicked out of the last place."

"Penny!" Dave dashed straight out from behind his cash register, arms wide. He embraced her warmly. "You're back! And you brought friends?"

"Cisco, Amelia, and Red." Penny pointed at each as she named them. "Meet Dave. He's got the best booze in town, *and* he's going to put us up for the night."

"I am?" Dave's grin widened. "Course I am! Plenty of space out on the property, as long as you don't mind a view to infinity when you sleep." He ducked his head to look at the door. "Doesn't look like rain, so it should be a great night."

"Fantastic." Penny slapped a palm against Dave's. "We're going to Mrs. Chu's for lunch. Do you want me to bring you back some noodles?"

"Nah, I'm doing that low-carb thing." He patted his staunch stomach. "Started yesterday. Probably gonna finish by tonight."

"You jobber." Penny reached for the door. "What time do you close up?"

"About four. Maybe three, seeing as I have something to do for a change." Dave shrugged, clearly unworried about adhering to the sign on the door that said the bottle shop's hours were 9-5.

"I'll see you back here at five to," Penny said. "Don't want the bottle-o to close before we stock up for the night."

"Don't worry about that, mate!" Dave waved goodbye. "Beer's on me!"

Once outside, Penny pointed to the door at the end of the row of shops. "That way for food," she said.

Red didn't wait for further explanation, diving forward to pull the rattling screen door open for his friends as he inhaled deeply. "I smell dumplings!"

Amelia whispered in Penny's ear before she slipped inside, "They don't have one of those cats, do they?"

Penny shook her head. "Nope. At least, she didn't have one last time I was here."

"Hello?" Red tapped the bell on the counter twice.

"I'm coming, I'm coming." Mrs. Chu shuffled out from

the back room, a cup of tea in one hand and half a sand-wich in the other. "Don't you know it's lunchtime?"

"That's why we're here, Mrs. Chu." Penny stepped out from behind Red's large frame so her old friend could see her.

Mrs. Chu squinted, then scowled. "You know better than to interrupt lunch, Penny. Is that Boots? I'm telling you now, if I see a single chewed-up rodent in my shop..."

"It's great to see you too," Penny replied with a grin. The old woman was only this sour to those she loved. With anyone else, she was simply cold and polite.

"Who are they?" Mrs. Chu gestured with her sandwich, ignoring the strip of lettuce that fell onto the counter. "Are they your American friends?"

Penny gave a quick round of introductions. "We go to the Academy together," she said by way of explanation.

"Which one are you going to marry?" Mrs. Chu took a large bite of her sandwich, her mouth working furiously as she chewed it.

Cisco choked. Red clapped him on the back while covering his own chortled cough. Amelia simply gave a prim smile and pointed at Penny's boyfriend.

Mrs. Chu continued chewing. After she finally swal-lowed her mouthful with a loud gulp, she looked him over. "He's a little short for you," she told Penny in a loud whisper.

"I'll take that under advisement," Penny said, suppressing her laughter. "Now that you've finished your lunch, may we order ours?"

"Young people. Humph. No respect for their elders. Back in my day, my father would have me whipped for insolence like that!" Regardless of her complaints, Mrs. Chu moved over and pressed a button on the ancient cash register, bringing it to life with a short beep. "What do you want?"

The four students quickly placed their orders, and Penny grabbed four Cokes from the dripping fridge. She put them on the counter. Boots wriggled off Penny's shoulders onto the floor, slithered to the fridge, and tapped her nose on the dripping wet glass.

"A strawberry milk?" Penny asked.

Boots nodded.

"We don't sell rats!" Mrs. Chu snapped. "Or raw eggs."

"Come on, Mrs. Chu." Penny placed a child-sized bottle of bright pink milk next to the soft drinks. "You know she doesn't eat stuff like that."

"Oh, and I suppose she doesn't eat raw fish, either?" Mrs. Chu looked down her nose at Boots, who had perked up at the mention of a favorite treat. "Twenty-eight-twenty."

Penny handed her credit card to the old Chinese woman.

Mrs. Chu gave her a sly smile. "Fifteen percent tip?"

Snorting, Penny shook her head. "This is Australia, Mrs. Chu. We don't tip here, remember?"

"Ha! You're American now, Penny. Americans tip! Fifteen percent!"

Penny haggled her down to five, not begrudging the extra charge, but knowing that if she agreed to fifteen, Mrs. Chu would try and sting her for twenty-five next time she visited.

Once she had paid, Penny gestured for her friends to

join her outside. "She doesn't like people hanging around when she cooks."

Penny leaned against the cool concrete wall and fanned her face with her hands. "I missed this weather."

"You *miss* it?" Amelia asked. She pointed to her hair, frizzy and curled from the humidity. "This weather *hates* me!"

"I like it," Red assured her. "It makes you look like a wild lass straight off the moors, as likely to stab her beau in the neck as kiss him."

"Dude, your taste in women is weird," Cisco said. He dodged Amelia's withering glare. "I didn't mean it like that, Amelia!"

"Are you okay?" Penny asked her. "The heat must really be getting to you. You didn't even punch him."

Amelia wiped a sheen of sweat off her brow. "Could you do it? I just don't have it in me right now."

Penny obliged, spinning around to throw a lazy fist at Cisco's arm.

He slipped away easily. "Ha, you missed."

"I wasn't even trying." A prickle of delight ran over Penny's skin as she slipped into a proper defensive stance, fists raised to protect her face, her legs loose and ready to move. "You wanna give me another go?"

Cisco immediately matched her stance. "Not really. You hurt when you punch."

"I'll try to be nice." Before Penny had finished speaking, she shot one fist out in a quick jab. Cisco easily dodged, but she hadn't intended to hit him. Not yet, anyway.

They circled each other, moving out onto the sticky

asphalt of the parking lot. Heat rose in shimmering waves, and the sun beat down on Penny's arms.

She took a step, then flicked up a leg. Cisco blocked the kick and the spinning back-fist that came after it. He edged back before jumping toward her in a scissor kick. Penny spun out of the way, landing a strike across his shoulders. She thrust a leg out, foot striking his side hard enough to make him stumble.

They parted, then came together in a flurry of punches, blocks, kicks, and spins, then separated again.

Cisco gave her a wicked grin. "Loser buys the drinks tonight."

"No way. Dave already said he'd get the tab." Penny waited until Cisco struck with a fist. She slapped it away with an open hand and spun behind him, using the momentum to plant a knife-hand strike in his left kidney. She dropped back, raising her fists again. "Winner gets a foot rub?"

Cisco chuckled and agreed. He feinted to the left, catching Penny out in her eagerness to spar. He jabbed at the opening she left, striking a shoulder, quickly followed by an elbow to her gut. Penny growled, kicked the back of his knee, and wrenched his arm up behind his back.

"I surrender!" Cisco gasped as she tightened her grip. "Mercy! I give up!"

Penny let his arm go, stepped back, and bowed deeply to their audience.

Sometime during the sparring session, Mrs. Chu had emerged from the shop. She stood watching, arms folded, lips pursed. "How many people are coming?" she asked.

Penny frowned, confused. "People for what?"

"The wedding." Mrs. Chu jutted her chin at Cisco. "He's short, but he will do. Mrs. Chu's Chinese Take-Away will cater your wedding. How many people?"

"I'll let you know," Penny said. The heat that flooded her face was from the sparring, she was sure. *Definitely just the sparring.*

"Dumplings on a wedding menu sounds amazing," Red gushed. "Are we invited, Penny? Cisco, can I be your best man?"

"Best man?" Cisco scoffed. He seemed awfully flushed from the heat, too. "More like man's best friend."

"Your lunch is ready." Mrs. Chu blocked the doorway, hands on her hips. She glared at Boots. "No. Rats!"

Boots chuckled a laugh and slithered between Mrs. Chu's feet. The old woman snorted and strode back inside to grab the two plastic bags packed high with takeout containers. "Don't forget your drinks. No refund if you leave without them!"

Red grabbed the food and Cisco juggled the cans of Coke.

"Where are we eating?" Amelia asked.

Penny pointed back to the car. "There's a rest stop just up from here. It's shady, and the dunnies aren't awful."

CHAPTER NINE

It was a fifteen-minute drive down a dirt road to get to Dave's place. The Barina did an admirable job of navigating the ruts and bumps in the dusty road, although Penny's jaw ached from the teeth-chattering ride by the time they arrived.

"Did the girlie drinks survive?" she asked Cisco as she climbed out of the car.

He hefted a six-pack of drinks, a brightly labeled combination of pineapple, coconut rum, and grenadine. "They got a little fizzy. We might have to open them last."

"Is it really a good idea to start the night on rum, and *then* move to the soft stuff?" Amelia asked, screwing up her face. "Apart from the fact that rum tastes awful unless you're already drunk."

"If you think rum is a hard drink, wait until Dave busts out the moonshine." Penny chuckled. "Don't get me wrong, it tastes great. Just don't let him mix it for you. I swear the guy puts three parts alcohol to one part mixer. A couple of his drinks, and we won't be able to drive home for a week without blowing over the limit."

"The more you tell me about Dave, the more I like him," Red said with a grin.

Penny led the way up the steps of the old Queenslander, but instead of knocking on the front door, she followed the verandah around the side to the back of the house. She cupped her hands around her mouth and hollered, "Dave!"

She was answered by the rumble of an engine and the squeaky toot of a horn. Looking toward the giant tin shed across the yard, Penny spotted Dave. He was driving a ride-on mower with a trailer attached to the back. He waved to them, the noise of the mower growing louder as he approached.

When he reached the porch, he turned the key and switched off the engine.

"Load her up, boys!" Dave called. He gestured to the trailer in the back, which held a large Esky, some pillows, and a duffel bag.

Red hefted one of the beer cartons into the trailer, and Cisco carefully set the six-pack of fruity drinks beside it, then laid down the spirit bottles. Red peeked into the Esky, his eyes widening with delight when it revealed slabs of red meat on Styrofoam trays, covered in catering wrap.

"Wow, that's a spread!" Cisco exclaimed.

Dave grinned. "When was the last time you had real Aussie-grown steak cooked on an open fire?"

Cisco shrugged. "Never. Well, not Australian-grown beef, anyway. It's been years since I've had a proper steak at a campout, though."

"It's gonna knock your socks off," Dave promised. He pointed to the trailer. "Hop in. I'll drive you down."

It wasn't a tiny trailer, but Penny still felt squished once the four of them had squeezed in beside the cooler and the drinks. "Are we going down by the creek?" she asked.

Dave nodded, starting the mower again. "Too damn hot for anything else," he yelled over the noisy motor. "Go for a swim, dry off by the fire, and drink the night away. It doesn't get better than that!"

Penny shared a contented glance with Cisco. "Sounds like we're in for a good night."

He grinned. "That's if I can even move after you beat me up before. I might just float downstream, waiting for you to tow me back to shore. You know, I thought you were going to dislocate my knee."

"I couldn't embarrass myself in front of Mrs. Chu," Penny protested. "She never would have let me live it down. Besides, now she approves of our relationship."

"I didn't realize that was a prerequisite for us being together," Cisco remarked.

"She's crazy, but she cares about me," Penny explained. "Then again, that goes for most of the people in this town."

"I'm beginning to see that," Cisco said with a knowing glance toward Dave. "I gotta tell you, this is the most fun I've ever had on vacation."

Penny shook her head. "We're not on holiday, remember? We've got a couple of nights of freedom, but then we're back on the job. Not to mention the exams we've got coming up."

Amelia winced. "Did you have to remind us about that? This semester has been crazy. Between the adventure we had rescuing Trevor, and then being scooped up to come to Australia?" She shook her head. "I can't believe they still expect us to take our exams."

Penny frowned. "That reminds me. Do any of you guys have your intake paperwork for next semester? I didn't before I left. It's normally sent out by now."

Red and Amelia shook their heads, but Cisco frowned. "Something is up with that.".

"What do you mean?" Red asked. As he spoke, he cracked open the carton of beer and pulled a few bottles out. He slipped them into the Esky, burying them deep in the ice to chill them for later.

Cisco hesitated before answering. "I'm not sure. I just know that the FBI has really been pushing Dean March to get this first bunch of students qualified and out in the field. I think they might be restructuring this last semester or something. I don't know details, just that Dean March is pretty pissed off about it all. She doesn't think we're ready."

Penny spent the rest of the trip in silence, musing about what that might mean. There was a very real probability that within the next six months, she and her friends would no longer be students at the Academy. Instead, they would be fully qualified FBI operatives, expected to hunt down and resolve conflicts with Mythers on a full-time basis. *There is still so much to learn*, she thought. *So much we don't know.*

Of course, the lecturers at the Academy didn't necessarily know much more either. She had known from the beginning that most of her learning would be on the job, out in the field, getting hands-on experience. She glanced at Boots, who gave her a comforting head butt on the jaw.

"What do you think, Boots?" Penny asked softly. Despite their noisy surroundings, Boots seemed to hear and understand her. "Are we ready for this?"

Boots nodded exuberantly.

The mower lurched to a halt, and Penny sprawled into Cisco's lap. Rather than help her up, he grinned cheekily. "You can stay if you want," he said.

Penny rolled her eyes and climbed out of the trailer. "Help me get this Esky out, will you?"

Cisco helped her heft the heavy cooler and carried it near the already crackling bonfire. He eyed the heat warily. "And to think, I thought it was hot before."

Penny shook her head. "It's disgusting during the day, but it can still get a bit nippy at night. You'll be glad of it later. Besides, you can't cook without a fire."

"I'm the one who's cooking," he insisted. "But I'd rather boil than bake. Where's the creek?"

***

Dave waved Penny and her friends off, insisting they go swim while he tended the fire. Penny led Cisco down the narrow track through the scrub that lined the waterway, dumping her bag beside the water. "Turn around."

The boys let Penny and Amelia change into swimsuits first, not bothering to do more than strip down to shorts. Penny waded into the water, pushing off as the sandy bottom dropped away. She lazily swam to the middle and drifted downstream a bit before swimming back to her friends.

"Where's my pool noodle?" Penny called.

Boots responded by spitting water into her face. Penny tweaked her tail, and the snake darted forward and wrapped Penny in a python's death grip. Penny let Boots pull her under the water, playing dead until the serpent let go in a huff. Boots nudged Penny's feet and guided her up to the surface in a whoosh. Penny, familiar with the trick, waited until her body broke the water before pushing off Boots' nose and launching into a flip, splashing back down into the water with glee.

"Woah!" Cisco clapped. "Boots, do me next?"

Penny swam over to Amelia and watched as the boys played with Boots, diving and flipping, and once, using Boots as a rope swing as she dangled from a branch hanging over the water.

"See?" Penny giggled. "She's a glorified pool noodle."

Shadows soon stretched over the water, and the air cooled enough to give Penny goosebumps.

When they returned to the makeshift camp, Dave had finished setting up and was sprawled by the fire beside one empty beer and one still full. The drinks were stacked by the Esky, pillows spread against a fat log, and some blankets were spread out over the ground.

Dave gestured at the accommodations. "It's no five-star hotel," he said with a shrug. "But you can't beat the view. Especially once the stars come out."

He was right. As afternoon turned to dusk and dusk turned to twilight, stars pierced the purple sky one by one. Embers from the fire flew up toward them, sweeping and twirling in the soft breeze.

Penny reached for another beer, but Dave waved her hand away. "Are we ready for the good stuff?"

"Sure," Penny said. "But I'll pour it myself, thanks."

"Look, I only made you throw up that one time. I didn't know you were so soft." Dave reached behind the log and pulled out two bottles, one filled with a clear liquid, the other bright purple.

"What the hell is that?" Penny asked skeptically.

Dave gave a proud grin. "I call it unicorn piss. It's basically gin with some fairy floss flavoring in it. Trust me, you'll love it."

He poured five shots and handed one out to everyone. Penny sniffed the sickly-sweet brew and wrinkled her nose. "I'm going to spend the rest of the night throwing up, aren't I?"

Dave shrugged. "I give you more credit than that, personally." He nodded at Red, who was staring at the fire with a dopey smile. "Not sure about your friend, though."

Amelia looked from Dave to Red, then plucked Red's shot glass out of his hand. "You have a point. I'm not cleaning up his mess tonight—or any night."

"I'm Irish," Red protested. "I can hold me drinks."

Penny squeezed her eyes closed, then threw the shot back. She almost spat it out again. "Dave, that's disgusting! I'm pretty sure *actual* unicorn piss would taste better."

"You've never met a unicorn," Dave said, tipping his head to one side. "Have you?"

"Damn straight, I have," Penny said proudly. "I raced it on a motorbike."

"Ah, come on, love. Not like you to tell a furphy." Dave shook his head, disappointed. "I saw you on old Mike Wallace's trail bike. No *way* were you racing anything on two wheels."

"She was pretty bad when we started," Cisco admitted. He caught Penny's offended punch, laughing. "You were! But you got the hang of it eventually."

"I could kick your ass in a race," Penny shot back.

Cisco snorted. "Don't bet on it. You're okay, but you're still not as good as me." He waved his hands to diffuse her outrage. "You can kick my ass on four wheels, that's a given. Just not on a bike."

Dave gave a low whistle. "Little Penny racin' around on a motorbike? That uni must be teaching you some pretty cool stuff."

"It's an Academy." Penny corrected him with a posh British accent and a wave of her hand.

"Oh, right." Dave grinned. "Graduated from the school of hard knocks, meself. Don't think I'd fit in at one of those *Academies*."

Penny waved away his statement. "You'd fit in fine. I mean, if I can not only share a room with a glitzy shopaholic but end up best mates with her, you would make friends with half the campus before the first week is out. And the classes aren't what you'd expect. There's book work, sure, but it's all old legends and myths. You know more stories than anyone I know! And the rest is practical, things like defensive driving, shooting, hand to hand combat..."

Red clapped a sloppy hand on Dave's shoulder. "Aye, she's right, mate. You might be a wee bit older than the rest of us, but you'd be welcome. You look like a practical man, and more importantly, you have a *lot* of booze. I've never seen anyone with so many bottles of liquor. We'd *love* to have you come visit!"

Dave patted Red's hand and poured him another drink. "You're a good one for an Irishman."

"Aye, I am." Red squinted at the sky, where stars clustered amongst the Milky Way across from a bloated half-moon. "Until the full moon. Then I turn into a right prick for a while."

Dave shot Penny a quizzical look, but before she could attempt to explain, he held up his hands. "Shh! You hear that?"

A scuffle in the nearby grass made the hairs on Penny's neck prickle. She slowly turned over onto hands and knees and peered over the fat log. "Is that a wallaby?" she asked in a whisper.

"Penny, what's wrong with it?" Amelia sounded worried.

The small mammal waddled a few steps in their direction, bright black eyes reflecting the firelight. Then, it turned and scurried away with an awkward gait. A stick dragged behind it, scraping over the ground.

"It's been shot!" Amelia hissed. "Penny, that poor creature has an arrow in its ass!"

She started forward, but Penny grabbed her arm. "No, don't chase it."

"We have to find out who did this." Amelia's face was set in a furious expression.

Penny shook her head. "I don't think anyone did. Amelia, I think that was a Myther."

"What?" Amelia pulled back, confused but ready to listen.

"He's a Dreamtime story," Dave said softly. "Like Boots."

"Tell us a shtory?" Red pleaded. He'd already slumped down into his seat, eyes half-shut.

"Penny?" Dave gestured to her, but she shook her head. "All right, then. I'll tell it."

The story he told was simple, like one for children. He spoke of the mountains and grasslands, and of two tail-less kangaroos that lived there. They had come upon each other as the smaller roo was eating honey from a hive in a hollow rock.

The larger one asked the small roo to share but was tricked into grabbing a handful of spiders instead.

"They fought, those roos, with big sticks, beating each other over the head until they'd both had enough. Then, as they turned and fled, they threw the sticks at each other. Well, the big roo caught the stick in his rump and so did the small one, but they were both too afraid to stop running, so they kept on with those big old branches stickin' out their backsides until…well, until they turned into tails." Dave shrugged. "That's the story we learned as kids, anyway. I did chat with an old Murri bloke once, though, and he said it's close enough."

"I remember reading it in school," Penny admitted. "But I'd forgotten a lot of the details."

"What about the Rainbow Serpent?" Cisco asked.

Penny told that one, with a few details to argue with Boots, who frequently interrupted with headbutts and exasperated coughs.

The rest of the evening was spent telling stories. They each took a turn sharing a childhood legend they'd grown up with—all except Red, who was snoring loudly on the other side of the fire.

When they had exhausted their memories and their energy, Penny snuggled into her sleeping bag next to Cisco.

"This has been amazing, Penny," he murmured. "I'm so glad I got to see your home."

"Could you live here?" She asked sleepily. "Not forever. I know you couldn't leave your mum and dad. But part-time, maybe?"

He smiled gently. "For you? Anything."

CHAPTER TEN

They stayed two nights at Dave's property, spending their days in the creek or snoozing under trees and the evenings telling stories under the stars. Even after they returned to the hotel, the brief interlude in Penny's hometown was enough to sustain the team's spirits until the call finally came.

"That Flying Crow Mythical Eco Adventure starts with a train ride on the Outback Magic," Crenel explained, handing them each a folder. "A two-day journey to a remote location in the Queensland rainforest. That's followed by four days in a 'state-of-the-art refuge for endangered magical creatures,' where you will 'interact with beings from ancient myths and impossible stories.'"

Crenel flicked away the brochure he'd been reading. "I managed to convince our contact to let us skip the vetting process."

"Vetting process?" Penny snorted. "Do they want to check that we're rich enough, or just completely lacking in morals?"

Crenel shook his head. "Neither. Remember, on the surface, this is all completely aboveboard. Whatever illegal trades are going down, they are happening out of the public eye."

"So, what do they need to vet?" Red asked, scratching his head.

"That we can *see* them." He gestured at Boots. "She looks amazing if you're one of the few who can *see* her. Those numbers are growing every day, but..." He shrugged.

"But a non-believer would be demanding a refund when it's done," Penny finished for him.

"Exactly." Crenel closed his folder. "We leave in the morning."

Penny eyed the plush chairs and ornate coffee tables in the lounge car. "This doesn't look like any train trip I've ever taken."

"Me either." Red dropped into one of the chairs and stretched. "It's nice! The wobbling takes a bit of getting used to, though." As if to prove his point, the train swayed a little harder as they rounded a corner. "Still better than watching some old drunk pissin' in the corner while a couple of biddies go at it with their brollies."

"What the hell kind of trains do you have in Ireland?" Cisco asked, bewildered.

"This says the dining car is two up from here." Amelia examined the flyer that detailed the train's offerings.

"There's a cafe and a bar. Oh! One of the carriages has a viewing deck above. Cool!"

"Where's the bar?" Red's ears perked up immediately. "And the food? I'm starving!"

"Red!" Penny exclaimed. "You ate *four* Big Macs for breakfast! You can't possibly…"

"He's close to the change," Amelia said. A hint of worry colored her voice. "The full moon is tomorrow night. His appetite will settle a bit after that."

"Crenel has it sorted." Red sounded unworried. "He's sneaking me food, and it might come in handy. Nothing like a nighttime recon mission with a superpowered sniffer!"

"Don't you dare," Amelia scolded him. "What if you get caught by a poacher? It's an operation that targets magical creatures, Red, and you're one of them!"

"Ah, it'll be fine, lass." Red plucked the flyer from her hands. "Or it will be if I can feed me grumbling tummy. Who's up for some grub?"

Penny offered to join him for a stroll to the cafe car, more to work off her restlessness than to fill her already-comfortable stomach. That quickly turned into the four of them making their way between excited patrons.

As Penny stepped through the connection between cars, she heard an unmistakable trill from behind.

"Penny? Gerald, don't you think that girl looks like Penny?"

"Oh, God, no," Penny mumbled. She tried to push ahead, but Red blocked her way.

"Penny, someone's calling you." Ever helpful, Red

gestured over Penny's head. "Aye, this is Penny. Look, Penny, that old lass is yelling your name."

Stifling a groan, Penny turned. "Hi, Mum."

———

Unable to find a way out of it, Penny eventually suggested her parents join them in the Outback Magic café car.

"What are you *doing* here?" she asked. "These tickets cost more than your car."

"Oh, we didn't pay for them. We won them at our local FLAPA chapter!" Penny's dad pouted. "It was the first prize. Bastards wouldn't let me swap them for the meat tray."

"You have a flapper chapter?" Amelia's eyes were wide with wonder. "That's *amazing.*"

"Yes, dear. Functional Level-Axis Proponents Australia." Marge, Penny's mother, handed Amelia a business card.

"It's a flat-Earther group," Penny said dryly. "Mum, I told you, don't get involved with those kooks. They're crazy!"

"Says the girl with the magic snake!" Gerald laughed. "Look, I'm not sure I believe all that nonsense, but you have to admit, there's a lot of crazy stuff going on out there, Penny my love. Who's to say they won't suddenly decide the world isn't round after all? I mean, they make new discoveries all the time!"

"Dad, that's not how it works." Penny sighed. "You know what? Never mind. You're crazy, both of you. Always have been."

"We?" Gerald leaned forward. "You mean your mum. Look, love, she's got a few roos loose in the top paddock but—"

"I know what that means!" Cisco looked immensely proud of himself. "By the time we're home, I'll speak fluent Australian."

"Enough about us, dear." Marge sipped her milk-white tea. "What are you and your friends doing here? I thought you said you were flying in to do something for the FBI. We certainly didn't expect to see you on holidays!"

"It's not a holiday, Mum." Penny bit her lip, unsure of how much she should disclose. Thankfully, she was rescued.

"Mr. and Mrs. Hingston?" Crenel leaned over to offer a hand to Gerald, who shook it after shaking off some crumbs from the scone he had just stuffed into his mouth.

Gerald gave a hard swallow, then nodded a greeting. "G'day, Mr. Crenel. I gotta say, we were surprised to see our Penny on the Outback Magic. Is this one of your secret missions?"

"Hush, dear." Marge swatted her husband's generous stomach. "If it is, you don't want to go blowing their cover!"

"You're as bad as he is, Mum." Penny covered her face and groaned. "Look, you really don't want to be here, okay? I can't tell you why. Just, when we get to the next station, go home. I can give you some money to cover the tickets, and I promise I'll take you on holiday as soon as this semester is over—"

"What?" Cisco interrupted. "Penny, you can't send them

away, we've only just met! It'll be fine. I mean, we're working, sure, but I want to get to know your parents." He gave Mrs. Hingston a winning grin and she blushed.

"How painfully do you want to die?" Penny hissed in his ear.

Cisco just shrugged. "You met mine."

"Yours are… Well, not a couple of flat-Earthers to start with." Penny appealed to Agent Crenel, who had watched the exchange with amusement. "Agent Crenel, they really should go home, shouldn't they?"

"It's probably best. For the integrity of our mission, if nothing else." Crenel leaned forward to confide in Mr. Hingston. "We're undercover. Very secret. Can't risk being exposed, if you know what I mean."

Gerald slapped Crenel's shoulder, making the agent wince. "No worries, Mr. Crenel. We'll keep it all under wraps. Very circumspect, we are."

Sensing that trying to argue with her father was a losing battle, Penny appealed to her mother. "Mum, please. This is really important. And dangerous!"

"I wouldn't say dangerous," Agent Crenel mused. "It's just a reconnaissance mission. We're only here to gather some information, remember?"

"That settles it." Marge carefully put her teacup back on the saucer. "If Agent Crenel doesn't think it's dangerous for us to stay, then we'll stay. Penny, we hardly see you anymore. We simply can't let this opportunity go."

Gerald patted his daughter's slumped shoulder. "It's all right, Penny-love. We won't mess up your super-secret mission. You won't even know we are here."

Penny lifted her face from her hands to offer the agent a glare. "You'll pay for this later," she told him.

Crenel just smiled. "I can't wait."

CHAPTER ELEVEN

To Penny's relief, the rest of the trip passed smoothly. Although her parents were never quite out of sight, and every time they caught her eye they waved madly at her, they did allow Penny and Cisco their personal space.

To be fair, there wasn't a lot of space on the train to start with. The rest of the day was spent meandering between the lounge car and the café, which Red frequented in an attempt to fill his growling stomach. He was the first through the door at four o'clock when the dining car opened.

He led Amelia past several tables covered in crisp white linen tablecloths adorned with sparkling silverware and crystal glasses.

"Why am I suddenly terrified I'm going to break something?" Penny whispered to Cisco as they made their way through the carriage.

Red slipped into a four-person booth, immediately picking up his cutlery and tapping impatiently on the table.

Amelia stilled his movement with one hand. "If you salivate any harder, you're going to ruin the tablecloth."

Red rolled his eyes but busied himself by picking up the menu and scanning the options. "Reef and beef… Ribs and rump… I wonder if they'll let me order both."

Amelia rolled her eyes. "I was going to get the seared salmon, but I guess I'm having steak, aren't I?"

Red wrapped an arm around her shoulders. "Thanks, love. I knew you'd have me back."

Penny had to admit, the menu did look appetizing. In the end, she couldn't resist a big fat juicy steak. "You get the salmon, Amelia. Red, do you want me to order ribs or seafood? I just want the steak."

Red grinned. "You're the best, Penny. The ribs, please."

Amelia gave Penny an appreciative grin and added a heartfelt thanks when their meals arrived. "This fish is cooked to perfection," she gushed.

"So is the steak," Penny moaned. She closed her eyes to savor the juicy mouthful. "You might have to fight me for your half, Red."

Red lifted his eyebrows in a mournful expression. "Don't say that, Penny. I'm so weak and hungry, you could beat me with one arm tied behind me back."

"Yeah, until the moon comes out tomorrow night and you rip my throat out for breaking a promise," Penny joked.

"You'd deserve it," Cisco said through a mouthful of pasta. "You don't promise a man ribs unless you mean it."

Red gave a deep sigh. "You don't have to share if you don't want to, Penny."

Penny laughed. "I was only joking, Red. Come on, I couldn't eat this much food in three days!"

The incredible meal put Penny in a good enough mood that she almost didn't mind when her parents slipped into the booth across from them.

"G'day, stranger! Long time no see!" Gerald tucked a corner of his napkin into the neck of his shirt. "How's the tucker?"

"Get the steak, Dad," Penny told him. "It's absolutely incredible."

"Where is Mr. Crenel?" Marge asked. "I was hoping to run into him again. He's done such a good job of keeping you safe, even if he did steal you away from home in the first place."

"He's busy," Penny said, not elaborating. "And he didn't steal me away from home. Not *your* home, anyway. I moved out two years before I went to America, Mum!"

"When I said home, I meant Australia. Australia is your home." Marge sighed. "America is such a long way away."

"I thought flat-Earthers all believed Australians were paid actors? That the whole country is just an elaborate hoax?" Red pointed out. "How's that work if you live there?"

"Well, *those* people are clearly idiots," Marge said. "Imagine thinking Australia isn't real!"

"Imagine thinking the world is flat," Penny mumbled, shoving more food in her mouth in the hopes it would keep her out of trouble with her parents.

"It's not that we believe the earth is flat," Gerald protested. "We're just open to the possibility. That's all. Just like we were open to the possibility that our daughter's best friend was something out of a fairytale she learned in primary school."

"Come on, Dad. That's not the same, and you know it." Penny reached for her drink, wishing she had an entire vat of unicorn piss to dull the assault on her brain cells.

"Look, there's Mr. Crenel again." Marge waved a hand and gestured the agent over. "Mr. Crenel, why don't you join us? There's plenty of room in our booth."

Crenel looked around desperately, but the nearby tables were all full.

Penny considered scooting over to make room for him to sit there, then remembered his idiot comment about their mission not being dangerous.

"Yeah, *Mr.* Crenel. Take a seat with my mum and dad." Penny smiled sweetly, ignoring the scowl she was gifted with in return.

"I'd love to." Crenel's voice was more growl than anything, but Marge didn't seem to notice.

She scooted over to make room for the agent. "Mr. Crenel, it's so good to have the chance to have a chinwag. My Penny is such a bright and clever girl, isn't she?"

Appetite gone, Penny shoved her plate toward Red. "I'm done." She grabbed her beer, tipped it back in a gulp, and stood. "Cisco. Bar. Now."

"Yes, dear." Cisco flashed a grin at Red and Amelia, then slid out of the booth to follow Penny.

"Can you believe them?" Penny seethed. "They're going to give him my whole life history. He's FBI *and* the Academy Liaison! He doesn't need to know that I took forever to ride a bike without training wheels, or that I was afraid of koalas when I was a kid!"

"You were afraid of koalas?" Cisco weathered the scathing glare admirably. "I just meant that I didn't pick that up when you were at the zoo."

"I was five, Cisco. I'm an adult now," Penny said. She covered her burning face with her hands. "They're just so…*embarrassing.*"

"Koalas are embarrassing?" Cisco motioned for the bartender, who nodded and finished up with his customer.

Penny shot him a dark look. "No, you idiot. My parents."

"What'll it be?" The bartender, whose name was Matt, according to his name tag, passed Penny a wine list. "Beer and house wine are included in your package, but hard spirits and boutique wines are extra."

Penny passed him the wine list without glancing at it. "Scotch. A good one. Actually, make it two, please."

"No problem." If Matt was surprised at her order, he didn't show it.

"And one for me." Cisco chuckled, jerking a thumb in Penny's direction. "That's if there's any left when she's done."

Penny snorted. "Don't be ridiculous."

"We don't have a magic hangover cure here, remember?" Cisco murmured in her ear.

Penny picked up both of her glasses. "Come and sit." She led Cisco to one of the high-backed chairs in the corner. The bar resembled a gentleman's club, with its old fashioned furniture and dim lighting. The only thing missing was the hazy scent of tobacco. "Look, my parents aren't always this weird."

"Hey, it's okay." Cisco patted her knee. "They're not *that* bad."

"They are," Penny insisted. "It's just that they don't get out much, or they never used to. Now they're retired and living the nomad life, they've suddenly realized that people exist outside of tiny farming towns. Mum knows Dad sticks out like a sore thumb, but she loves him, so she joins in the madness. And he just wants to show her the world."

"That's kinda sweet," Cisco admitted.

Penny sighed. "Yeah, until they bail up my future job reference and try to show him my baby photos."

Cisco smirked. "At least it was just Crenel. Could you imagine if we'd had to bring Dean March? She'd be beside herself!"

Penny giggled. "Dean March and flat-Earthers? Oh, *hell*, no. I can already see that big pulsing vein in her temple. It'd explode!"

Cisco chortled. "I'm not sure if she'd completely erupt or just stand up and walk out with that glassy expression that means she's off to rip into her husband."

"I wonder if she'd throw me out of the Academy after meeting them?"

"What, and lose their best student?" Cisco frowned at Penny's eye roll. "You do know that, right?"

"Know what?" Penny asked.

"You're March's top student. The best all-arounder." Cisco grinned. "I'm third on the ladder after Trevor, and Amelia and Red are right up there too. But you? The FBI can't *wait* to get their hands on you."

"What?" The praise made Penny uncomfortable. She knew she was a good student. She worked her ass off, just like her friends did. It was the comparison to her boyfriend that rankled her a little. "You do heaps of stuff better than I do," she insisted.

"You've got the thing," Cisco said quietly. A hint of pride warmed his voice. "That thing that makes a good agent. We all see it. You're special, Penny."

Waving away the compliment, Penny finished her first scotch. "Rubbish. We're all special. And so is this scotch, *wow*. Even Paddy would be impressed!"

When Penny awoke the next morning, it took her a moment to get her bearings. She sat up in the narrow bunk and rubbed her eyes, glaring at the slice of dim light Boots was letting in through the gap she was making in the curtains.

Penny groaned. "Boots, what are you doing?"

Boots dropped back to the floor, letting the curtain fully close. She slithered back to Penny's bed and began tugging her blankets down.

Amelia leaned down from the top bunk. "Is it raining?"

Penny nodded. "It doesn't look heavy, but I can't see an inch of blue sky out there."

Amelia sighed. "Yet again, my wardrobe is proving to be woefully inadequate for this trip. You didn't happen to bring a spare raincoat, did you?"

"Sure," Penny said. "I always have an emergency poncho in my bag, and I packed my Driza-Bone for the trip."

"I never thought I'd have to rely on you for clothes," Amelia admitted. "What are you going to wear?"

Boots chuckled at that and nudged a pair of jeans out of Penny's bag.

"Right," Amelia said dryly. "Jeans, a t-shirt, and those ugly-ass boots. I don't know why I needed to ask."

"It *has* been a year and a half," Penny pointed out. She wriggled out of her pajamas and began to dress. "You really should know by now."

Boots pulled herself up to the top bunk and buried herself under Amelia's blankets. She popped her head out the top and booped Amelia's nose.

"Okay, okay. I'm getting up." Amelia rolled off the bunk and landed with a thud, then stumbled as she found her balance on the swaying train. "I can't wait until we arrive. I'm so sick of this trip."

"It hasn't been so bad," Penny said. "The food is great."

"Penny, you spent all of yesterday trying to hide from your parents. On a train. There's nowhere to go!" Amelia rifled through her bag, and after some consideration, also pulled out a pair of jeans. "Or did you finally sneak off to get some privacy with Cisco?"

"We mostly just hung out at the bar," Penny said. "It's nice in there. Not too crowded."

Amelia rolled her eyes. "I spent the afternoon following Red around to every carriage with food on offer. I'll be shocked if they have anything left for breakfast this morning."

Thankfully Amelia's fears were unfounded. When the girls arrived at the dining car, a full buffet breakfast had been laid out. "This looks amazing," Penny gushed. "Look, they even catered for Americans!" She pointed toward a jug of maple syrup next to a plate of steaming bacon and stacks of thick, fluffy, freshly-made pancakes.

"You know, I think it's actually a Canadian thing we adopted. They put maple syrup on everything. Hell, they probably eat their shirt if they spill syrup on it." Despite her words, Amelia quickly added a few strips of bacon to her plate and drizzled some syrup over them. She added a pancake, then scanned the room for coffee.

By the time the boys joined them, Amelia and Penny sat before empty plates and mugs.

"You ate without us!" Red complained.

"Yes, I ate. It's nice to do that occasionally and not have half your meal stolen by a hungry boyfriend." Amelia smiled to take any sting out of her words and picked up her empty plate. "I don't mind going for a second helping, though."

"And you'll share it with me?" Red asked. "There's no way I can fill my tummy with a single plateful of food. I don't even think two would do."

"Dude, you really need to get that sorted." Cisco rubbed his eyes. "Your stomach was growling all night. It was so loud it kept me up."

"You go grab some food, and I'll get you a coffee," Penny offered. "Can you get me an extra pancake? With some bacon and syrup? It tastes so good."

Cisco kissed her on the forehead. "Anything for you, my dear."

"You're making me jealous," Amelia teased. "The sharing of food only runs one way in our relationship."

"Aww, Milly, you know I'd never let you starve." Red

wrapped an arm around his girlfriend. "I'd let me stomach eat me from the inside out if it came to that."

"I know you would, you big goof. Come on, let's go fill your rumbly tummy." Amelia led the way over to the buffet, with Red and Cisco trailing behind her.

CHAPTER TWELVE

The train arrived at their destination mid-morning. Penny stared out the window of the lounge car, wondering what the hell they were in for.

"Oh, look at that." Whatever Marge pointed to was obscured by her face, pressed against the window. "It's like a big tent! Not one of those rubbish pergolas, a big fancy one. Oh, I can't wait!"

"Mum, are you sure you want to go through with this?" Penny asked. "I don't want you and Dad to get hurt. It's not too late to go home."

"Now Penny, don't forget, me and your mum are as old as the hills. I know you think this uni of yours has taught you everything you need to know about life, but we've been around the block a few times." Gerald gave his daughter a suffocating embrace. "We'll be just fine, your mum and me. We'll stay out of trouble, and we'll be super careful not to blow your cover."

"Not talking about blowing our cover would be a really great start, Dad," Penny groaned. Still, she hugged him back. "Look, I'm gonna be pretty busy while we're here. I'll try and catch up for dinners, okay?"

"Of course, dear." Marge patted her arm. "I'll do my best to keep your dad out of your way. We've got a holiday to enjoy!"

Penny watched her parents make for the exit, arguing over who packed the charging cord for the camera, and if anyone had locked the laundry door before they left. She felt a pang of homesickness and promised herself she would make time for them before the trip was over.

She slung a backpack over one shoulder, then coaxed Boots inside. For now, the serpent was to stay hidden. Penny didn't want to risk her being targeted by whatever operation they were here to investigate. "I promise to let you out to have some fun later."

Penny stepped off the train and hurried over to the enormous shelter. It wasn't just any tent. A big steel beam supported the centers, holding taut the thick white fabric pinned to the ground by heavy ropes. Tourists clustered inside, and Penny noted at least a dozen new faces, all dressed in matching uniforms embroidered with a white crow on the left breast. One such person approached them.

The black of his uniform matched his glossy black hair, the green trim vibrant against his dark skin. His eyes glittered as he approached.

"Good morning!" The man gave them a warm smile. "My name is Corey. I'm going to be your assistant today. I'll give you a quick tour of your accommodations, then show you to the restaurant for lunch. Is this all of your party?"

Penny glanced at her friends, then scanned the crowd. "We're waiting for one more." Red, Amelia, and Cisco were beside her. Off in the distance, she could see her parents chatting excitedly to one of the other hosts. Agent Crenel, however, was nowhere to be seen. "Anyone know where he is?"

"Dad probably has some business to attend to," Cisco said pointedly. "I'm sure he'll catch up."

Corey smiled in understanding. "We can wait for your father to join us if you like, or go on ahead. Our staff will look after him, I promise."

When Penny gestured for him to go ahead, Corey led them through the crowd to the other side of the tent. Rain-splattered walkways led toward several buildings, each named after an Australian native animal. Checking the names on his clipboard, Corey informed them they would be in the Wombat residence. He passed each of them a small package of folded plastic. "Ponchos, so you don't get wet."

Amelia opened hers excitedly. "I won't have to borrow one, Penny." She slipped her head through the opening, bunched up the sleeves, and twirled. "Honestly? It looks like a plastic bag."

"It *is* a plastic bag," Penny agreed. "But it's waterproof and tiny."

"If you damage or lose it, don't worry," Corey reassured her. "We have plenty. You'll find them by the doors at most of the buildings, along with complimentary umbrellas."

"Can I get a hand with mine?" Red asked dubiously.

Penny looked at him, then burst into giggles. He'd managed to get it on all right—in a manner of speaking. The "one size fits all" designation apparently hadn't taken Red's enormous size into account. Even before he'd contracted lycanthropy, he had been taller and more muscular than most. Now, however, he was a giant. Penny realized she had stopped noticing until he got into situations like this one.

The plastic stretched and warped over his chest and bunched up around his biceps. One sleeve, in fact, had already split open. Red-faced, he stood there with his arms out, trying not to do any more damage.

Struggling to keep a straight face, Corey offered to run for an umbrella.

"Naw, it's just rain," Red said. He gave up trying to keep the poncho in one piece. He flexed, stretched, and shook. Pieces of the poncho drifted to the ground while he gently tore off a sleeve that still clung to his body. Bunching it into a ball, he looked around for a trash can. "Oh, hey! Look who I found!"

Agent Crenel was loitering around the trash can, talking on his phone. When he saw the students gesturing at him, he quickly ended his call. "Hey, kids! Sorry, I got a bit lost back there. Have you found our rooms yet?"

"Corey was going to take us over," Penny explained. "We were just waiting for Red to finish destroying his rain gear."

Agent Crenel eyed the plastic packet Corey offered him, then shook his head. "It's just a sprinkle. I'll be fine."

"Now you're all together, let's go find your rooms." Corey ducked out from under the cover of the waxed cloth roof and into the rain. With a quick glance to check all of his charges were following, he led the way to the accommodation area.

"Rooms" was a bit of an overstatement, but not by

much. Rather than traditional cabins or cottages, the resort accommodation was in the form of luxurious glamping tents. They were tall enough to stand up in, assembled on wooden floorboards, and came complete with electricity and running water.

"It's a tiny house made out of cloth," Amelia gushed, impressed. "We're roughing it without an ounce of rough."

"Doesn't look anything like roughing it to me," Penny said. If she was honest, she would rather be sleeping under the stars at Dave's. This wasn't a holiday, though, and she had to admit it was a lot nicer than some of the cheap hotels she had stayed at.

"Your luggage will be delivered in the next twenty minutes," Corey said. "Do you remember the restaurant building I pointed out on the way here?" Penny and Amelia both nodded. "You'll need to meet there for lunch at midday. You can certainly head over earlier if you like, but we do request all guests be present for the introduction and the safety briefing. We wouldn't want any of you to get eaten, now would we?" Corey gave an exaggerated wink, then asked if there was anything else the girls needed.

"We're good," Penny assured him.

"Right then. I'll go and make sure your friends are settling in, then meet you in the restaurant at midday. If you need anything before then, that's where I'll be." Corey ducked out of the tent, closing the flap behind him.

"I wonder how safe that is," Amelia mused. "If this place really is full of Mythers, is that flimsy cloth really going to offer any protection?"

"Let's hope we don't find out," Penny said. She jumped when somebody tapped at the tent flap. "Who is it?"

"Santa Claus." Crenel peeled the flap up and stuck his head in. "We need to talk."

"I just got off the phone to one of my contacts," Crenel said brusquely. "Something isn't adding up."

"What kind of something?" Penny asked. She unzipped her backpack so Boots could join the conversation.

"Looks like Silas might be involved after all." Crenel shook his head, clearly unhappy with the development.

"Silas? You mean Geoffrey Nevins' brother?" Amelia said. "The one you swore *wouldn't* be involved?"

"Exactly." Crenel reached for a cigarette, then looked at the soft wall coverings and put it away. "Dammit. Look, I'm not sure either way yet. Our information is coming through my superiors at the FBI, who are getting it through Interpol, who are getting it from God *knows* where. It's a clusterfuck of Chinese whispers, and we're on the butt end of the joke. Whoever is on the Australian end is apparently putting up a fight thanks to our involvement at the zoo."

"What?" Penny shook her head, confused. "Why would they do that?"

"Oh, I don't know…" Crenel screwed up his face. "Getting shown up on their own soil, the meddling involvement of a foreign agency. Take your pick."

"If we can't trust the information we've been given, we may as well be going in blind," Penny pointed out.

"Worse." Crenel crossed his arms, his stance mimicking the dissatisfied look on his face. "That information can lull us into a sense of false security. Some of the worst mistakes I've seen on the field were because of people relying on information they shouldn't have. At the same time, we can't disregard it completely. Stay on your toes, keep out of trouble, find out what you can."

"Staying out of trouble isn't exactly our specialty," Amelia teased the agent. "But we'll do our best."

"Good. What's your plan?" Crenel waited expectantly.

Penny gestured to the open tent flap and beyond. "Be tourists. Do the tour, catalog any and every Myther we see, and match those up to the ones we know were procured before the trading ban. Cross-reference those with any known to be poached or kidnapped. And, you know, be tourists. Stick our noses in where we're not wanted, poke around where we shouldn't, and generally make nuisances of ourselves."

Crenel gave a brisk nod. "There seems to be a general lack of stupidity in that plan. I like it."

"Our plans are never stupid," Amelia protested. "They just…well, don't always pan out."

"That's the understatement of the year," Penny muttered. She turned a bright smile toward Agent Crenel. "We have an hour until lunch. Plenty of time for us to get into trouble. Are you coming?"

He lifted a skeptical eyebrow. "What do you think?"

Penny grinned. "I *think* I'll see you at midday on the dot, hopefully talking to my parents and keeping them out of trouble."

After Agent Crenel left, Penny looked at Amelia. "So, where is our first stop?" She tossed one of the brochures toward her friend and gestured at the map on it.

Amelia studied for a moment. "The gift shop."

"Seriously? I know you love shopping, but—"

Cutting her off, Amelia explained, "If they're trafficking animals illegally, who's to say they're not also selling forbidden artifacts?"

"Oh. Sorry." Penny grabbed her purse and gave Boots a quick scratch under the chin. "Are you coming with us? You'll have to stay hidden. The backpack probably won't do." She held out a water bottle enticingly.

Boots shook her head, burying herself under the pillow on Penny's bed instead. Soon, the only part of her that was visible was the tip of her tail.

"You could have just said no." Penny set the water bottle on the small table next to the bed. She left the lid off in case Boots was thirsty, then headed for the tent flap. Once she and Amelia were both outside, Penny fastened it. "This doesn't feel very secure. What if someone goes into our room and sees Boots?"

"It'll be fine. Boots knows to hide if she hears someone coming. Worst case scenario, she eats them whole." Amelia gave a shrug. "You know if it comes to that, they'll deserve it."

"You're right." Penny gestured around her as they walked toward the buildings they had passed on the way to their room. "It's just that all this is not what I was expecting. I didn't think it would be so nice. Or so…"

"Touristy?" Amelia held up the brochure. "There's a whole page on this thing about eco-conservation and a big spiel about how the goal is to *prevent* the poaching and exploitation of Mythers. Not the kind of thing you'd expect from the very people who are doing that."

"They didn't send us here on a hunch," Penny pointed out. "The FBI must've had some kind of concrete information to send us here. There has to be something going on. Besides, when you think about it, wouldn't that be the perfect cover?"

"Then let's find out what the real story is." Amelia pushed against the glass doors of the gift shop. "Starting right here."

Not for the first time that day, Penny was taken by surprise. She had half-expected to find taxidermied Mythers on keychains and lanterns fueled by sprites trapped in glass jars. Instead, the gift shop specialized in art pieces. There were already a couple of guests meandering through the expensive display, ogling framed photographs of rare Mythers and pointing at tapestries depicting ancient gods and legends.

One corner in particular drew Penny's eye. A cluster of artwork—photographs, paintings, and bright wooden carvings—depicted creatures from the Dreamtime stories. The centerpiece was an oil painting of a giant rainbow serpent basking by the side of a creek. The artist had done an excellent job of recreating the way the sunlight shimmered on bright scales and had somehow captured an element of intelligence in the glittering black eyes.

"It's beautiful," Penny whispered.

"It's my favorite piece."

Startled, Penny spun toward the voice. The gift shop attendee—at least, he was wearing a Flying Crow uniform —stared back at her, expressionless.

"It's very pretty. Have you ever seen one yourself?" Penny asked.

"Of course." The attendee turned to a nearby shelf and began tidying it. "There's one in the amphibian tank. You'll get to see that tomorrow. It's small, though. Not as majestic as that one."

"Right," Penny muttered. The thought of seeing another rainbow serpent unsettled her. Despite knowing that her presence here would ultimately protect animals being snatched up from the wild and sold on the black market, she wasn't entirely sure she could keep her mouth shut if there was another Boots here, trapped in a cage for the enjoyment of spectators. Of course, speaking up wasn't an option either. Not unless she wanted to blow the whole operation.

"I think it's time for lunch." Amelia grabbed Penny's arm firmly and steered her out of the shop. "We'll come back and look at the pretty pictures later."

Once they were outside, Penny shot her a grateful grin. "That was intense," she admitted.

Amelia grimaced. "I could tell. Penny, you're going to have to do a better job of hiding your feelings. You looked like you were about to murder that poor guy!"

"As if he noticed," Penny scoffed. "The guy looked bored out of his brain."

"Shall we head to the restaurant?" Amelia flicked a glance at her watch. "The safety presentation starts in twenty minutes. If we get there early, we should be able to get a good seat."

Penny nodded and let Amelia guide her toward another building, this one set back amongst the trees and separated from the rest of the compound by a shallow, babbling brook. A fat green frog sat by the water, chuckling away.

"Is that frog *laughing*?" Amelia paused on the footbridge. "I mean, actually *laughing*? Like Boots does."

"It must be Tiddalik," Penny said in awe. "He's a Dream-time legend, just like Boots. He drank all the water and created a big drought. It wasn't until another creature made him laugh that he opened his mouth and brought all the water back."

"An awful lot of your legends vomit water," Amelia said, screwing up her face.

Laughing, Penny continued toward the restaurant. "I dare you to complain about that in front of Boots."

"She's already drowned one pair of shoes. I'm not going to put another on the firing line." Amelia paused. "Or is that watering line?" She shook the thought off and pushed open the restaurant door.

Penny inhaled the rich aroma that flooded out. "Coffee."

"Definitely not a coffee line." Amelia glanced at her friend. "Though I swear, given the chance, you'd have an IV of the stuff hooked up to you twenty-four seven."

"And you wouldn't?" Penny didn't wait for an answer. Instead, she headed for the coffee machine in the corner. Rather than a push-button self-serve dispenser, a barista stood behind an expensive espresso machine.

Penny inhaled the aroma and smiled. "Now *this* is service. Can I grab a latte, please?"

"Make that two." Amelia ignored Penny's triumphant smirk. "Where's this safety thing being held?"

The barista gestured over a cloud of steam, pointing toward the long table in the middle of the room. "They might be running a bit late," she explained when the hiss of the milk frother ended. "Sam normally gives it, but he's been called out to an emergency."

"Right." As Penny watched her coffee being poured, she briefly wondered if she had time to investigate that emergency.

Amelia nudged her elbow. "Come on, let's go sit down."

"What about Sam?" Penny asked in a low voice. "What do you think he's up to?"

"Probably tracking down someone's lost luggage," Amelia said firmly. "Even if we wanted to check it out, we have no idea where he is or how to get there, even if we did!"

"Fine." Penny slid into a seat down one end of the banquet table and sipped her coffee. It was *good*. "I guess I can live with my curiosity unsated. My God, this coffee is amazing."

"It's probably that fancy stuff that gets pooped out by civet cats," Amelia said with a bright grin. She giggled when Penny snorted, clutched her nose, and glared over her napkin. "Hey, it's a thing! Probably not *this* thing, but it exists!"

"Way to ruin an amazing coffee," Penny muttered. She took another tentative sip anyway. "You know what? I don't care if it *is* cat crap coffee." She jumped when someone appeared next to her.

The employee smiled sweetly. "Oh no, that's not Kopi Luwak."

"Kopi what?" Penny asked, confused for a moment. The woman next to her looked like Corey, their host. It wasn't just her glossy black hair or dark skin. It was her eyes, deep brown and glittering with mischief. *Maybe they're siblings,*

Penny guessed. She was even more disconcerted by the woman's name tag. *Who'd name their kids Corey and Cora?*

"Civet cat poop," Cora clarified.

"Thank goodness." Relieved, Penny sipped her drink again.

"It's Wild Bat Geisha coffee. It's processed by bats. Not cats." Cora spun and strode off to a back room, leaving Penny to eye her latte with distaste.

"If you spit that out, I'm never taking you out in public again," Amelia warned her.

Penny swallowed her mouthful with a hard gulp. "I noticed you've stopped drinking yours."

"Penny, it was *pooped out by bats*," Amelia hissed. "Of course I'm not drinking it. That's disgusting!"

"What's disgusting?" Red pulled a chair out next to Amelia. Before he sat, he took a long drink of the steaming hot coffee in his hands.

Penny tried not to let her horror show on her face. "You know that cat-poop coffee?"

Red nodded and took another sip.

"That's what you're drinking," Amelia said. "Well, it was crapped out by bats, not cats. Either way, you have poop in your mouth, Red. I'm never kissing you again."

Red made a point of continuing to drink his coffee. When he finally put it down, he chuckled. "Whoever told you that was pulling your leg. I watched the barista fill the grinder. They use the same cheap generic stuff we were drinking at the hotel."

"No way." Penny reached over and picked up Red's cup. She took a sip, then shuddered. "It doesn't taste remotely the same."

"Aye. It's the milk that makes the difference. Some fancy organic cold-pressed brew, with all the cream still in it." Red plucked his coffee cup back out of Penny's hands. "Had a good old chat with the coffee lad about it."

"Why would someone who works here tell us it was made from poop?" Penny looked around to see if she could spot the employee who had stopped by the table. There was no sign of her. "That's just mean!"

"Are you sure you're not having me on?" Red teased. "Maybe she was just trying to upsell the garbage coffee beans."

Amelia shrugged. She picked up her coffee cup, examining it through narrowed eyes, then took another tentative sip, closed her eyes, and whispered, "It's not poop. It's *not* poop."

"It's really not." Red seemed perplexed by the entire conversation. He looked around the rapidly filling restaurant, then waved a hand. "Cisco, can you help me convince the girls this coffee isn't made out of shite?"

Cisco ducked around a small cluster of guests and made his way over to the table. "I had one before, and it tastes fantastic! Don't you like it, Penny?"

"Never mind," Penny grumbled. "Hey, it's almost twelve. I wonder when the safety thing is going to start?"

They didn't have to wait long. Three hostesses hurried out, none of them Cora, and distributed a stack of menus, setting one at each place at the table regardless of whether it had been taken. By the time they were done, most of the seats had been filled.

A well-dressed woman walked to the head of the table, stood behind a chair, and clinked a spoon on a glass. Her simple white blouse and green slacks looked well-made but not ostentatious.

"Welcome, guests." She beamed a sunny smile at those watching. "We'll try to keep this short. It's terribly boring, and I'm sure you're all itching to get to the fun stuff." There was a smattering of laughter at that. "My name is Sophie, and I'll be presenting the safety briefing for you today. Normally, Sam would be giving this presentation. Unfortunately, he's been called away to an emergency. You see, many of the creatures you will come across on our property—real or mythological—have been rescued. Some were bought off the black market to keep them out of the hands of poachers who would harvest the creatures for their skin and bones. Some were found in areas they were simply not designed to live in. Others came to us injured and required treatment in our state-of-the-art treatment center for wild Mythers. Once rehabilitated, we do our best to find homes for those creatures in their natural habitat."

She paused, growing somber. "Sadly, that's not always possible. In the case of highly-sought-after creatures, it's often too dangerous for them to be out in the wild, unprotected. That's why we exist."

"Is that why you don't sell dragon's balls in the gift shop?" one of the guests called, laughing.

Sophie smiled gently. "You certainly won't find any animal parts for sale here. On the rare occasion that we are unable to save one of our emergency rescues, the body is cremated. The Flying Crow Eco Refuge will never take part in anything that could bring these creatures danger."

"You said you bought them on the black market, though?" Penny's voice cut through the approving mutters of her fellow guests. "Isn't that just encouraging more money to trade hands? Increasing demand?"

"In those cases, we don't operate alone," Sophie explained with a small smile. "The Australian Federal police are always informed. With our help, they have arrested and charged nine smugglers of mythical creatures in the last two years. Most are let back into the wild or returned to the tribes they were created by. My own people, the Uw Oykangand, reclaimed a Rainbow Serpent thanks to Sam's hard work up here."

Penny sat back in her seat, lips pursed. "Those guys have an answer for everything," she mumbled.

"Of course, there are risks that come with interacting with wild creatures. Whether they are real or mythological, it makes no difference." Sophie waited until she had everybody's full attention. "It is absolutely imperative that you obey all instructions given to you by your guides. When approaching fenced areas, do not attempt to climb over or push your fingers through the wire. Although our most dangerous creatures have been double-fenced, there is always a tiny risk our first layer of defense has been breached. We want you going home with all of your fingers and toes intact." She smiled brightly, but her tone made it clear that she was deadly serious. "There is signage around the property with more specific instructions. Anyone seen to be disobeying those will unfortunately have to be ejected from the property. There is to be absolutely no feeding of mythical creatures you encounter, or regular animals for that matter. Rest assured, each species you will encounter is being fed a highly specialized diet to keep them in the best of health. The only exception to that is within the designated area where hand feeding is allowed, and even then, please do not offer the creatures human food. You will be provided with bags of a special dietary mix that is suitable for the animals you will encounter."

The instructions were all sensible, the sort you are heard at any regular zoo. In fact, Penny had read most of them in the brochure during their earlier visit to Sydney Zoo.

"Curfew is seven PM," Sophie continued. "Don't worry, you won't be trapped in your tents. You may travel between the residential areas, the restaurant, and the other buildings, just not out into the refuge."

"I can't decide whether that's a sensible safety precaution or a sign that they've got something to hide after dark," Penny whispered to Amelia.

"And finally," Sophie continued, "it is absolutely forbidden to take anything with you when you leave apart from what you brought in or purchased at the gift shop. The animals, Mythers, and even much of the flora here have been carefully selected to live in harmony. Though it may seem harmless to take a small souvenir, the risk of disease transmission or unintended harm coming to whatever you take is too high. As per your contract, all bags and belongings will be checked before you leave."

Sophie smiled again and spread her hands. "And that's it! See, I told you it wouldn't be too long, even though it was a little boring."

"When will we get to see the animals?" someone asked.

Before Sophie could answer, she was interrupted by another question. "Why isn't there any meat on this menu? I could murder a good steak."

Penny cringed, immediately recognizing Gerald's voice.

Sophie gave a winning grin at someone toward the front of the long table. Penny leaned forward and was just able to make out her father's profile.

"As we mentioned in the contract and all of our promotional materials and on the *really* big sign hanging at the front door, the Flying Crow restaurant provides meat-free meals to our patrons. Don't worry, we're not vegan. There's milk for your coffees, butter for your toast, and even ice cream for dessert." Sophie held up a hand to forestall the complaint Penny was sure was coming. "I highly suggest the Korean barbecue stir fry if you want a good, hearty meal. The tacos are delicious as well, and the vegetable pot pie should fill even the most discerning stomach. Any other questions?"

Penny couldn't hear her father's grumble, but she did hear Marge's sharp response. "Don't get your knickers in a twist now, Gerald. There's lots of nice food on this menu, and it's only for a few days. You know the doctor said you should cut down on red meat. Well, now's your chance."

Penny sank her face into her hands, not for the first time on this trip. "Kill me now."

To Penny's shock, Gerald struck up a conversation with someone else about the menu. "How about you, Mr. Crenel? You look like a man who might enjoy a good rack of ribs."

"Absolutely," Crenel agreed. "The barbecue stir fry does look tempting, though. Not too heavy for lunch, but tasty."

"Why is he sitting with my parents?" Penny hissed. "Bastard. I bet he's trying to get baby photos out of them. For leverage."

"I'm pretty sure it's illegal for an FBI agent to blackmail someone," Cisco pointed out. "But if he tries, I'll take him down for you. Just let me know where you want me to hide the body."

"You're not getting your hands on those damn photos either," Penny said, jabbing a finger toward Cisco.

Cisco shrugged. "It was worth a try."

CHAPTER THIRTEEN

The first tour offered by the Flying Crow Refuge was that afternoon. The guide Benny was an Islander man in bright orange board shorts and a shirt dot-painted with a colorful frog. After introducing himself, he led the group of interested guests toward what looked like the stretch limousines of golf carts.

"Sorry 'bout the weather, folks." Benny pointed at the roiling clouds in the sky. "Our transport might be covered, but you're gonna get wet if it rains. Don't say I didn't warn you!"

"How does this thing run?" Cisco asked. He slipped into a seat next to Penny. Red and Amelia crammed in after him, squashing the four of them in tightly. "I hope we're not going around any sharp corners. The damn thing might snap in half."

Despite Cisco's misgivings, the vehicle ambled along without any trouble. They took a route that wove into the rainforest, bumping over tree roots and winding around gentle curves as Benny rambled on like any good tour guide would. He pointed out vibrant lorikeets flitting among the treetops and slowed the vehicle right down so that everyone had a chance to see the brilliant green python lazily wrapped around a tree branch. What really piqued Penny's interest, though, was when they trundled over the log bridge that spanned a gently flowing creek. The vehicle stopped, the gently idling engine drowned out by squawking birds and bubbling water. Penny reached out of the cart to feel the mist rising from the water, only to realize it was coming from above. It had started to rain.

"How many of you know the story of Tiddilik?" Benny's voice carried easily over the ambient noises of the rainforest.

He told the story Penny was already vaguely familiar with. She, along with most other Australian schoolkids, had learned the story in her younger grades. When the native Australian man told it, however, Penny felt like she could see it unfold before her very eyes. Benny's tale was rich and detailed in a way that Penny had never heard it before. *Makes sense,* she mused. They only taught the kid's version in school. As she lost herself to the story, her eyes drifted to the water below. She blinked when a tiny, vibrant flash of rainbow streaked through the water.

"Did you see that?" she asked Cisco.

He tore his eyes away from the trees. "The giant frog? I swear, I almost could. This guy tells one hell of a story!"

Penny watched the water carefully, but whatever she had seen, it didn't come back. It must've been a trick of the light.

Benny finished the tale of Tiddilik and the long cart lurched into motion again. They stopped twice more, once by a cave filled with ancient paintings, and once at an outcropping that looked down into a ravine. Both times, Benny told stories from the first of the generations that had lived in the area. He painted a rich picture of life before technology, of oral traditions passed down by the fire and history recorded with burnt sticks on stone walls.

The second story he told was a more recent one from Australia's past. Benny sang *Waltzing Matilda* in a soft and haunting voice, explaining the story behind it.

"Do you mean to tell me," Amelia asked Penny, "that Australian kids sing nursery rhymes about the suicide of a sheep thief?"

Penny shrugged. "It's better than singing about the black plague. Come on, you know most nursery rhymes have really horrible meanings behind them."

"I guess I thought Australia was just...nicer." Amelia shuddered as Benny wrapped up his story.

"There are some who believe the billabong in Banjo Patterson's song is this one right here. That belief is so strong that now with the tearing of the veil, you can hear the ghost of the swagman singing his song if you listen closely."

There was silence in the coach, and Penny found herself straining her ears to catch a hint of the spooky tune. She heard nothing.

Benny chuckled. "Just joking, folks." The motor chugged to life again as the cart continued forward. "We're off to an underwater extravaganza!"

He pulled up a short distance ahead and ushered the tourists off the vehicle and onto a tiny path. Penny hung back, letting the other tourists meander ahead. She shivered as the trail led into a dark tunnel.

"This is clearly manmade," she noted to Cisco. Filtered light shone through opaque skylights overhead, but the cloud cover made the underground cave damp and dark.

"And here you'll see some of the aquatic creatures that live at the refuge." Benny waited at a bend in the path. Penny gave him a brief smile, then gasped as she turned her head to see where they had arrived.

The tunnel was lined on one side by thick Perspex that created a window into the creek that flowed alongside it. Penny spotted a platypus digging through the rocks and a few fish, but quickly forgot them when she saw Boots.

Except, it wasn't Boots. This serpent was smaller, and although it frolicked happily in the water, coming up to show off in front of its spectators, Penny easily guessed it didn't have the level of sentient intelligence Boots displayed.

"A Rainbow Serpent," Benny proudly told his audience. "She's not the only one in the country or even the state, but she's ours. Pretty little thing, isn't she?"

"How do you keep her secured?" Penny asked, her mind already ticking over methods of breaking it out.

"Secure?" Benny frowned in confusion, then laughed. "No, love. This isn't a zoo. She comes and goes as she pleases. We don't keep her here."

"Then how did you know she'd *be* here?" Penny asked.

"She likes the attention!" Benny pressed his hand against the heavy plastic window and the serpent butted against it. "Sometimes she's not in the mood, but there's always a few platypuses or eels to look at. She's usually here, though."

The rain began to fall in earnest as the cart traveled back to the resort. Thunder rumbled in the distance, and Penny shivered. Cisco slipped an arm around her. She snuggled closer to him, her skin warming against his.

"Lucky I brought a raincoat," Penny murmured. "Pity it's still in my room."

"It'll probably clear up by tomorrow," Cisco replied. "With any luck, you won't need it."

"Tomorrow?" Penny pulled back to look at him, the twinkle of excitement in her eye. "Forget tomorrow. That curfew is a screaming invitation to go and poke around after dark."

"Tonight?" Cisco glanced at Red, then looked back at Penny. "Are you sure that's a good idea?"

"I'll be fine, ya big worrywart. Besides, this cloud cover might make the whole thing a non-event." Red leaned across the aisle to whisper loudly at Cisco. "Even if it clears, my control is really good these days. It'll help if I can get out and do something useful while I'm…uh… He turned to look at an older woman who had stretched up in her seat, paying rapt attention to the conversation. "Flatulating."

The woman sat back, disgusted, and Red shot Penny a wolfish grin.

"Really? Flatulating?" Amelia sat back in her seat, arms crossed. "I can't take you anywhere."

"You've said that, but you still keep taking me places." Red didn't seem thrilled with that reality.

"How did he even hear us talking?" Cisco spoke so quietly, Penny almost didn't hear him at all.

"Supersonic hearing." Red wiggled his index fingers by his ears. "I'm super-juiced today."

"Clearly." Penny smirked, then dropped her voice in case the nosy old lady behind them was still eavesdropping. "At least I know who to take with me on my little adventure tonight."

Red gave two thumbs-up and a wink. "I can't wait."

Penny turned her eyes to the refuge. They were almost back at the departure point now. Her smile widened as she realized just how much she was looking forward to some real fieldwork.

The resort itinerary listed a formal welcome dinner at six that night, exactly the kind of event Penny was perfectly happy to skip in favor of a sneaky recon mission. Agent Crenel, however, had other plans. His text message came as Penny was laying her clothes out on the bed.

Dinner in thirty. Sit at the table closest to the large window. Don't be late.

Amelia looked at Penny's outfit—black cotton drill pants, a navy t-shirt, and a heavy belt with clips to attach basic tools and weapons. "That won't do for dinner."

"No kidding." Penny yanked her bag open and rifled through it until she found what she was looking for. "How about this?"

The dress was simple but elegant. Green silk hung loosely from carefully placed silver rings on the shoulders, dipping low at the front so that it almost showed her belly button. Amelia recognized it immediately, which made sense, seeing as she was the one who had insisted Penny bring it.

"Yes!" She tossed her slinky number aside and ran up to grab the dress. She held it against Penny, nodding. "Shoes?"

Penny hesitated. "Uhh…"

"You forgot to bring shoes to go with it?" Amelia shook her head in disgust. "You guys make so much fun of all the stuff I bought, but you're lucky I did. I just *happen* to have a pair of silver pumps that'll go perfectly with this."

"Thank you." Penny hugged her. "I promise never to make fun of your oversized baggage again."

In the end, Penny had to borrow not just shoes, but a hair straightener and half a roll of dress tape. "I feel like I'm being held together like a kid's craft project," she admitted, patting the plunging neckline again to make sure it was secure. "I really wish I'd thought about things like sitting and walking before I bought this rotten thing."

"You're being ridiculous." Amelia closed her eyes as she wafted a long stream of hairspray over her head. When she was done, she gave Penny a knowing look. "It'll be worth it. You'll see."

It was entirely worth it for Penny when she saw the look on Cisco's face. The last-minute change in plans had made the two girls a little late to the dinner, so it was one of the rare occasions Cisco had arrived first. The young man stared as his girlfriend approached, jaw hanging so low it was in danger of being stepped on.

"Penny?" Cisco almost choked on her name. "You look amazing!"

"Thanks." Penny moved closer and dropped her voice. "How's Red? Is he…"

"Fine." Cisco snorted. "He's lying in bed watching YouTube on his phone. It's cloudy out, and he said the change won't happen unless it clears."

"I'm glad he didn't show up anyway," Amelia said as she slid into her chair. "It *would* be just like him to take a stupid risk like that."

"Girls." Crenel dipped his head in greeting, then glanced at his watch. "Glad to see you finally made it."

"Yeah, well, I'd made other plans," Penny told him. "You know it takes more than thirty minutes to look like this, right?"

He shrugged. "I can't say I've ever gone through the process."

"Yoo-hoo! Penny!"

The sound of her mother's voice immediately took Penny from feeling like a sophisticated adult back to her high school days, when Marge would waltz into the school calling her daughter's name, asking anyone in earshot where she should take a forgotten homework folder.

"Over here, Mr. and Mrs. Hingston." Crenel gave Penny a winning smile. "I invited them to join us."

Penny gave a long-suffering sigh. "Could you give me a little warning next time?"

"You can sit next to me, Mrs. Hingston," Cisco offered. "Have you seen the menu? It looks really good."

"It's not more of that vegan rubbish, is it?" Gerald asked.

His wife tutted disapprovingly. "Now, Gerald. We

talked about this, remember? You promised me that you were going to start trying new foods. Besides, remember what the doctor said about your bowels? You *need* to start eating some vegetables!"

"Oh, for God's sake Mum, please don't talk about Dad's bowels at the table." Penny glared at her mother, who shrugged.

"Dr. Smith told him, he said, if you don't start getting more fiber in your diet—"

"Marge, love, I promise not to complain about the food again." Gerald gave Penny a reassuring grin. "Can't you see you're embarrassing the poor kid?"

"Oh." Marge suddenly seemed to remember there were other people at the table. "I suppose we can talk about it when we get back to our room." She picked up a menu and began perusing it, making little sounds of delight as she went.

Glad the spectacle was over, Penny picked up her own. "Risotto." She folded it shut and placed it back on the table impatiently.

Cisco was still reading out the appetizers under his breath. He looked at her in surprise. "Penny, you barely opened it. There is some really nice stuff in here!"

"I did too!" Penny protested. "But really, can you ever go wrong with risotto? It's the perfect food."

"Too right." Gerald set his menu down on the table. "It'll never be as good as Marge's, but it'll do for dinner." Marge raised an eyebrow and opened her mouth to say something, but Gerald quickly added, "With one of those tiny salads on the side. Gotta have my vegetables, after all." He winked at his wife. Seeming mollified, Marge settled back in her chair, eventually choosing a fried tofu dish.

While the rest of the table decided what to eat for dinner, Penny glanced at the empty chair at the end of the table. "Is someone else joining us?"

Agent Crenel didn't look up from his menu, but a sly grin crept across his face. "Perhaps."

Penny's question was soon answered. A sandy-haired man arrived at their table, greeting them jovially before taking a seat.

"Welcome to the Flying Crow," he said with a grin. "I'm Sam. Sorry we didn't get to meet earlier. I'm normally here to give the safety briefing, but I was called away on an emergency rescue."

Before Penny could press him for details, Gerald cut her off. "G'day, Sam. My name is Gerald, and this is my wife Marge. That's my daughter Penny over there."

Penny's stomach dropped to her boots, and she rubbed a hand over her aching forehead. Her father had just blown their cover completely.

"Never mind," Agent Crenel murmured in her ear. "We can come up with something else later."

Between them, Gerald and Marge introduced everyone at the table. To Penny's relief, they remembered to refer to the special agent as Mr. Crenel.

"Thank God for small favors," Penny muttered to Cisco.

"You know, this could work out for the better." Cisco made a minute gesture toward Penny's mother, who had launched into a dozen questions about the "emergency rescue" Sam had mentioned. "Just wait and see."

Penny had to admit, her mother's natural curiosity and

complete lack of filters made her the perfect person to grill Sam for information. She sat back and watched the conversation, listening to Sam's story about the capture and eventual release of a local panther. Meanwhile, she tried to figure out which brother he was. He had too much hair for the older one and was too, well, clean-cut for the vegan terrorist.

"But panthers aren't magical," Gerald pointed out.

"Not normally," Sam admitted. "But for some reason, they seem to pop up in urban legends a lot. There's one here, and one a ways down south. Rumors about a crashed circus train, or an escapee from a zoo. Even I thought it might be real for a while!"

"Hang on, how do you know it's a Myther?" Cisco asked.

Sam steepled his fingers, his expression deepening to one that reminded Penny of their professors back at the Academy. "The rumors are mostly believed by people who have never seen a real live panther. All they have to go on is what they *think* a panther looks like and a whole lot of blurry pictures that may or may not be the rumored animal."

"So it looks a bit like a panther, but it isn't one?" Cisco's line of questioning was a good one. The Academy had taught the students that Myther versions of real animals often had telltale signs, like too-big teeth or simplified body structures. It seemed Sam knew that much, at least.

The story held up to scrutiny, at least on the surface. Penny couldn't fault his description of the Myther he had rescued, or his willingness to let the animal free in a less populated area to live its life out in peace.

Assuming he's not lying about that bit. For all we know, he rescued the poor thing then sold it on the black market.

"How did you find out about it?" Penny asked. "Are you the go-to guy for mythological events around here?"

"You could say that." Sam grinned, baring his sparkling white teeth in a way that felt a little *too* friendly to Penny. "I've built myself up a bit of a reputation. When things go wrong and there is a Myther involved, I'm the one they call."

"You're just a magical Steve Irwin, aren't you?" Penny chirped. She had to work to keep the vitriol out of her voice. This guy bugged her, the way he was sucking up to guests who were paying through the nose to fund what they thought was a charitable venture. If Penny hadn't known what the guy was really doing, she would have been sucked in too. It irked her instincts not to trust him since he was just that goddamn charming.

"I've always wanted a Myther as a pet." Cisco leaned back in his chair casually. "Can you imagine how much fun that would be?"

"Like tropical birds and rare animals, I much prefer to see them in their natural environment." Sam placed his hands carefully on the table, his chair sliding smoothly over the carpet as he stood. "Now, as much as I'd like to stay and chat, I need to go do the social thing. Enjoy your dinner."

Crenel waited until the man had gone before speaking. "I think you scared him off, Cisco."

"Creep," Penny muttered.

"What? Penny, he was nothing but polite to you. Quite

the charmer, in fact." Marge waved an accusatory finger at her daughter. "I've taught you better manners than that."

Penny blushed, sinking further into her seat. "Sorry, Mum." She couldn't fill Marge in on what Sam was suspected of. She loved her parents, but she knew they wouldn't be able to keep a secret of that size for more than a minute.

"Look, here comes our dinner." Gerald picked up the cotton napkin beside him and tucked one corner into his shirt collar.

Penny saw Cora walking toward them. Her uniform was still pristine, but now she had a gleaming black feather perched in her hair.

When Cora proffered a plate of steaming risotto, Gerald pointed at Penny. "Mine has the mushrooms, thanks, love."

After the meals were distributed, Cora looked at her watch. "Only an hour and forty-two minutes until the clouds part."

"What?" Cisco shoved a forkful of food into his mouth. "How do you know that?" he mumbled around the fragrant rice.

"We have a weather clock out back." She turned to go. "There are all sorts of magical things lurking around this place. You never know what might pop out of a bottle or around a corner."

CHAPTER FOURTEEN

When dinner was finally over, Penny all but ran back to her room. By the time Amelia caught up to her, Penny had already slipped out of the slinky green dress and was wriggling into more comfortable clothes. Boots rolled in the shiny fabric, clearly enjoying the feel of it against her scales.

Amelia perched on the side of her bed. "I don't know how you still have any energy left. I'm exhausted!"

"You don't need to come with me." Penny tugged the t-shirt over her head. "I'm going to be sneaking around in the dark. If it's only me, I'm less likely to be seen."

Amelia kicked her feet back and forth dubiously. "But what if something happens?" She thought for a minute, then set her face and determination. She stood and began to go through her bags. "I'm not letting you go alone."

"I won't be alone." Penny gestured toward Boots. "You'll come, won't you, Boots?"

Boots stopped mid-writhe, lifting her head. She nodded, then went back to cavorting on the bed.

"I have no doubt Boots would do anything within her power to keep you safe, but it's not like she can phone me if something goes wrong." Amelia shook her head. "I'm going."

"What if I go with her instead?" The tent flap pulled back, and Red's head appeared with a wolfish grin. He quickly stepped inside and zipped it shut behind him. "I didn't mean to eavesdrop, but I can hear every damn conversation in a thirty-yard radius."

"I don't know if you should be going anywhere in your state." Amelia folded her arms, staring down her boyfriend.

Penny had to admit, she had never seen Red this agitated.

He bounced on the balls of his feet, hands thrust in his pockets as his eyes darted around nervously. "The clouds are going to clear soon. I can feel it, Amelia."

"Red, you look like a tweaker. Can you stop bouncing?" Penny sat on the edge of her bed to pull her socks on. Cora's weather prediction had stuck in her head since dinner. "Say the clouds *do* clear. What if someone sees you turn?"

"I thought the whole point of a clandestine mission was to *not* be seen by anyone." Red shrugged, the movement quick and jerky. "Look, if I don't work off some steam, I'm going to go mad. You can use my skills. I'll be able to hear anyone coming. If anyone sees me, I'll just look like one of those dingoes running around."

"You've either never seen a dingo, or never looked in the mirror in your werewolf form." Penny couldn't help but laugh. "Wolf-Red looks *nothing* like a dingo. Not even a red dingo. Not even a little bit. But I don't mind if you tag along—if it's okay with Amelia."

"She's my girlfriend, not my mum." Red stole a glance at the woman in question. "But I'm sure she knows how much I want to go and wouldn't ask me not to."

Amelia rolled her eyes dramatically. "You're right, I'm not your mom. Nor am I a full-blown idiot, so it makes sense for you to ask for my advice every now and then." She folded her arms and tapped her chin, thinking. "Your points are reasonable. I think you should go."

Red's grin widened. "Thanks, Mum."

"That's gross, babe. Don't call me that." Amelia flopped onto the bed. "When Superdog freaks out at the enormous rumbling sound, you can tell him it's just me. In about five minutes, I'll be fast asleep and snoring loudly." She kicked off her shoes, not bothering to change out of her dress.

Penny finished lacing up her boots, then stood. She patted her belt, where she had already clipped her most vital equipment. "Are we ready to go?"

"Oh, *boy*, are we ready." Red ducked back out of the tent, coming to a halt outside to turn his face up to the soft glow of the sky.

Boots hissed happily. Penny reached an arm out, and Boots climbed it. A moment later, the serpent was curled around Penny's shoulders.

A soft silver glow edged the receding clouds, revealing the open sky above. Penny guessed they were only minutes from seeing the moon peeking out from its hiding place. A quick glance at her watch and some hurried mental math added up to a surprising and somewhat worrying fact. The waitress had been right to the minute about the clouds parting.

She didn't stop to discuss it with Red, hurrying instead along the neat path away from the sleeping quarters. Most of the tents were still lit up inside, and shadows moved against the bright canvas walls. She spied a small, dark building and jogged toward it, planning to use it for cover. The noise from behind made her turn.

Red had stopped. The noise was the belt buckle he had undone before unzipping his pants.

"Jesus, Red!" Penny slapped a hand over her eyes. "Can you warn me next time?"

"Sorry." Red's voice was a deep growl.

Penny turned her back on her friend to give him privacy—if such a thing was possible for a tall, naked man standing out in the open under the full moon. She heard him kick his jeans aside and tried to ignore the odd grunting that came after. She waited patiently until a cold nose touched her hand. She snatched it away with a yelp, then cursed at the shaggy red dog beside her. "Don't scare me like that!" she hissed.

The dog whimpered an apology, sitting back on its haunches to wait for Penny's instructions.

Penny shrugged at him. "I don't know where I'm going. You're the one with the super schnoz. Any ideas?"

Red gave a quick shake of his head. When Penny looked at Boots, the serpent did the same.

Penny sighed. "Fat lot of use you two are."

The small building she had stopped by was unlocked. It was stacked with paper towels and tiny bottles of organic toiletries. She didn't waste any more time looking through the neatly stacked boxes. Outside, the path she had followed away from the sleeping quarters continued, winding through a scattering of palm trees and off into the rainforest.

Penny pulled the resort map from her back pocket. Though its colors were washed out in the silver moonlight, she could still read it well enough to see where they were headed. "The wildlife hospital. I think that deserves a visit."

She let Red take the lead, knowing that he would be the first to pick up any movement nearby. Boots joined him, rolling off Penny's shoulders and landing on the leaf-strewn ground with a plop before slithering ahead. The serpent's abundant energy suggested she was well and truly sick of being cooped up in the tiny room and was enjoying the chance to stretch her legs. Her scales? *I don't even know how to parse that into serpent language.*

The wildlife hospital was not one of the attractions listed in the promotional materials. On approach, Penny saw that it was clearly not designed for casual visits by curious onlookers. A bland white building lit by two bright spotlights sat in a clearing in the rainforest. The chain-link fence that surrounded the facility was at least eight feet high and topped with barbed wire. Thin strips of electrical fencing tape surrounded the perimeter two feet apart, forming a wall. Whatever this place was, they weren't encouraging visitors.

"I wonder how much of that is to keep people out and how much is to keep something in," Penny wondered. "Red, can you dig under?"

Red pawed some of the loose dirt and leaves away from the base of the fence, revealing solid concrete underneath.

He looked back up at Penny, tongue lolling out one side of his mouth as he panted happily.

The spotlights were directed at the front of the building, but a third pointing at the rear had blown a bulb. It left the back conveniently cloaked in darkness. Penny headed in that direction, keeping to the shadows and moving as quickly and quietly as she could. Once she was out of the direct glare of the spotlights, Penny's confidence lifted a notch. She dropped to her belly and ducked under the lowest strip of fencing tape. With her face pressed against the ground, she carefully used her wire cutters to snip through the chain wire. She had only cut through three sections before Boots took a chance, slipping through the small opening Penny had created.

"Don't you dare sneak off without me," Penny hissed.

She supposed she could have sent Boots in for reconnaissance, but she wasn't sure the serpent would know what to look for. Penny wasn't sure either. If the building was a hospital, it could just as easily be for the genuine treatment of the refuge's animals as a holding center for smuggled Mythers. Still, even if Penny had evidence of the latter, she didn't plan to act on it. Her goal was to take photos and document everything she found. All they needed was enough proof to turn it over to the FBI. Then they could go in, all guns blazing.

Red dropped to his stomach and wriggled through the hole in the fence in a canine commando crawl. Penny followed him, her heart lurching when she snagged on the electric fence outside. Thankfully, it was just the rubber sole of her boot that had touched it. She pulled herself through and rolled to a crouch, then quickly scurried to the back of the building. She waited for a moment, her breath coming hard and fast, more from the adrenaline and excitement than from physical exertion.

There were no doors on the side of the building, but Penny spied two windows and a vent. A cursory examination of the windows was fruitless. The heavy glass was protected by thin mesh, with thick bars overlaying that. Although she could possibly smash it and create a hole big enough for Boots to pass through, there was no way Penny was getting in through that opening. Her eyes turned to the vent.

She could just touch the bottom of it. The kit strapped to her belt held a multitool, and she flipped out a screwdriver that matched the screws securing the vent in place. Penny went to her tiptoes and felt her way along the bottom of the metal plate with her fingertips, using them to guide the screwdriver into the slot on the screw head. Straining to reach the height, she jammed the screwdriver in and turned it. The first screw came out easily and dropped to the ground. The second wasn't as cooperative. The building was old, and a patina of rust had accumulated around the screw head. When Penny tried to undo it, she realized it had affected the screw. The screwdriver ground against the slot, stripping the head. Penny rocked back onto her heels in frustration.

"Dammit." She looked at Red and Boots, who were both staring up at her patiently. "I'm going to have to make some noise."

Her friends glanced at each other, then silently moved away. Boots went to the left of the building, Red to the right. Both stayed low, peeking around the corner to watch for anyone approaching. Penny held her breath for a moment, waiting until each of them had looked back and given her a quick nod.

Penny opened her kit again, secured the multitool back into place, and pulled out a thin chisel and a small metal plate. She used her left hand to position the chisel so its sharp point poked under the edge of the grate, pointed at the screw. The plate nestled on the heel of her right hand, protecting it as she rammed it into the end of the chisel.

It wasn't a perfect solution, but her third strike hit true. The screw snapped, and the bottom of the vent flapped free. Although Penny couldn't reach the top screws, the vent was flimsy enough for her to simply bend back. Of course, that still left the problem of getting inside it.

Penny opened the makeshift hatch as far as she could. "Red! Get over here."

The werewolf padded over and looked up at Penny's handiwork. He whimpered and took three steps backward.

"Don't be such a baby." Penny crouched and linked her hands. "Here, I'll give you a boost."

Red was surprisingly heavy. Penny hadn't expected him to be a lightweight. As dogs went, he was huge, but she had underestimated the amount of muscle he was packing under that scruffy fur. She grunted as she heaved him up, wondering if it was possible for him to weigh more than he did in his human form. Then again, he *had* put on a ton of muscle since contracting the lycanthropy virus.

With a desperate scrabble of claws on metal, Red managed to pull himself into the vent. It creaked and groaned as he wriggled along it, making Penny wonder if she should be worried about it collapsing under his weight.

Something clutched Penny's leg, and she looked down. "Oh, you want a lift too, do you?" She hoisted Boots up, and the serpent disappeared into the vent.

"My turn." Penny slipped her tool case back onto her belt, clenched her flashlight between her teeth, hooked her fingers over the edge, and gave a little jump. She pulled herself up to the lip of the vent, then made her way up to her elbows. With a grunt, she was in. This time, the pause to catch her breath was definitely from exertion. Penny wriggled her arms up to her front and clicked the flashlight on. It highlighted a mass of scruffy red fur...and a naked butthole inches away from her face.

"Go," she whispered. "And I swear to God, if you fart while we're in here, I'll hand you over to the poachers without a second thought."

The wolf huffed and scooted forward. Penny wriggled through behind him, passing several junctions in favor of going straight ahead until they both came to a dead stop. Red sniffed at something ahead, then lunged forward. Penny winced at the clatter he caused, then breathed a sigh of relief when she was suddenly alone in the vent. She edged forward and looked out into what looked like a medical supply room. A damaged trolley slowly rolled toward the wall.

Wishing it was as easy to get out of air vents in real life as it was in the movies, Penny lowered herself down to the floor headfirst. She used a shelf to support her weight and flipped onto the floor. Brushing her hands on her shirt, she grinned at the tail-wagging werewolf. "We made it in! Where is Boots?"

There was a hiss from the door, and Penny bowed

when it swung open. Boots waved her through with a flick of her tail.

The wildlife hospital wasn't a large building. The door led to a short corridor with three doors on either side and one at the end. If Penny's bearings were correct, the one at the end led to the front of the building. She headed that way first, only to pull back when teeth gently tugged at her wrist.

"What is it?" Penny whispered.

Red scampered back to the supply room, Boots weaving between his feet to race him in there. Penny hurried to follow and pushed the door shut behind her, making sure to hold the handle down so it closed silently.

Another door clicked open. "It was probably a possum," a voice said. "There's a whole family of them living in the roof. I keep telling Sam to set out traps, but you know how it is."

The door clicked closed again, and whatever response the speaker got was too muffled for Penny to make out.

"Thank God for that," she said, leaning against the wall. "I owe you one, Wolf-Boy."

Red snorted at the nickname and pointed his nose at the door.

"We're good to go?" Penny asked to confirm. Red nodded. "Right. Let's start at the end that's *not* full of people who would skin us alive if they found us here, hey?"

Boots was already hanging off the doorknob. She opened it with a flick of her tail. Penny moved faster this time, conscious that the door at the end of the corridor could open again at any moment. She paused at the next door just long enough to press her ear against it, but Red butted her out of the way. His claws scratched at the door as he flipped the handle and nosed it open.

"That's right, I forgot." Penny slipped in behind him, waited for Boots' tail to pass through, and closed the door again. "No point in me trying to eavesdrop when you've got super-hearing. Hey, if you happen to overhear any conversations while we're here, will you remember them when you shift back?"

Red tossed his head in lieu of a nod, and Penny got the canine version of an eye roll.

Penny looked around the room, which was an operating theatre. A large metal table stood in the middle of the room, surrounded by electronic monitoring equipment and trays for surgical implements. Penny shuddered, realizing the scalpels, tiny pliers, and other surgical instruments could easily do just as much harm as good. She picked up one of the tools, noting that it was immaculately clean. A quick search of the room revealed nothing else of interest. Nothing was present that would seem out of place in an everyday veterinary surgery. Nevertheless, she slipped out her phone and took photos of everything she saw.

"Next door, or across the hall?" Penny asked. Red lifted a paw and pointed. "Across the hall it is then. Boots, you'd make an excellent butler." Penny noted as Boots swung the door open for her again.

It only took a second to dart across the hallway. When she tried to open the door, however, it was locked. Penny hissed a curse and immediately set to work with her lock-picking equipment. The lock snicked open just as Red gave her a sharp poke with his nose. Penny slipped inside, and the wolf almost barreled her over in his haste to get inside.

The door clicked shut behind Penny just as another one in the hallway squeaked open. Penny held her breath as footsteps approached. When they faded again, she blew out a slow breath and looked around the room.

The back wall of the room was lined with cages. There was an aquarium along one wall, its water murky enough that whatever lived in it looked like nothing more than a dark shadow flitting back and forth. A second tank, this one set up as a terrarium, was sitting next to the door they had entered through. Beyond it was another door, one that would lead back out into the corridor.

Red walked over to the largest cage. Something large and black slammed against the wire door, then retreated back into the shadows as the werewolf whimpered.

"Yikes," Penny muttered. "How about we don't disturb the wildlife, Red? I'm not pulling you out of the jaws of a hungry panther."

Penny grabbed her phone out and began snapping pictures of the trapped beasts. A fox slapped its tail on the metal, sending a shower of sparks into the air. *I swear I've seen that one in a textbook somewhere, but I can't remember what it's called.* Beside it, she recognized a snotling—a gnome-like Myther with green skin that sat morosely in the corner of its cell.

The third cage held a machine, but Penny couldn't tell what it was at first. Gears and levers were linked together, and a broken spring poked out one side. "Gremlin," she whispered. The spirits often inhabited machines, breaking them beyond repair. The Academy had lost two printers, an ancient fax machine, and four laptops to a stray gremlin once.

Avoiding the large cage whose occupant had lashed out at Red, Penny approached the other end. Inside the biggest cell on that side, a deer had curled up into a comfortable corner, buried in blankets. When it saw Penny, it lifted its head and attempted to stand. One of its front legs, which were not deer legs but clawed like a large bird's, was bandaged.

"No, precious, sit down. Rest that leg." Penny crooned softly, and the creature dropped back down to resume its nap.

She went back to the others she had taken pictures of. The fox yawned as she passed, showing off a recently stitched lip and a missing tooth. The snotling sniffled and blew its oversized nose on a tiny handkerchief.

There was only one more cage to check. Unfortunately, she wasn't going to get the chance. Red scrambled to his feet, whining. For the second time during their adventure, Penny heard the tell-tale sounds of someone approaching. Even as her mind raced to find an escape, a key jingled in the lock to the second door.

Hsssss. Boots had reared up and was making a show of dominance at the largest cage.

"Now is not the time, Boots!" Penny hissed back. "We have to get out of here. We have to hide!"

To Penny's horror, a black, leathery claw reached out of the cage. It fiddled with the lock, claws scratching and clicking, and the door swung open.

"Oh, *no*. Boots! What have you done?" Penny tried to

back away, her fear of the approaching staff suddenly seeming not such a big deal.

Boots grabbed the hem of Penny's jeans between her teeth and tugged her toward the cage. She gave Red a hiss, muffled by a mouthful of fabric. He whimpered, shook his head, and backed away.

"Dammit." The voice outside the door sounded frustrated. "Why won't it open?"

Penny gulped. Boots nudged her toward the open cage again.

"They can't get in, Boots. We're fine," Penny squeaked.

"Just use the other door," a second voice called. "I told Sam the lock is stripped on this one."

Boots curled around Penny, lifted up to head height, and hissed loudly.

"Fine!" Penny squeezed her eyes shut and sucked in a breath. When she looked at the cage again, the shadowy figure had bunched up into one corner. She crouched and edged toward the cage. "Uhh, sorry. My snake said…well, you know. Please, *please* don't eat me."

She crept into the cage, curling up as tight as she could. The shadowy figure enveloped her in bony limbs that didn't quite match to the form she saw with her eyes. A claw reached out and gently closed the cage door. It clicked shut.

The door to the room swung open. "Was that door even locked? Jesus. I'm gonna kill Sam. He seriously needs to start fixing shit around here!"

"Yeah, I'm sure he'll get right on it. Do you *know* how long the coffee machine in the break room has been broken?"

Penny couldn't see the speaker since a dark cloud obscured her vision.

"Peter, a coffee machine isn't quite the same as basic security. Can you imagine what would happen if the media found out about the stuff we're keeping in here?"

"Speaking of our unusual residents, when did the dog arrive?" Penny heard footsteps pass her hiding place. A moment later, her cage-mate shifted so she could see.

Not that her view of two pairs of loafers and some jeans cuffs did much to explain what the hell was going on.

"Christ, Lucy, don't open it. He might be rabid!"

"We don't have rabies in Australia, you tosser. Anyway, he seems friendly." Lucy cooed softly, and Penny heard panting.

A cage door rattled as though someone was patting it. "Whatever." Peter sighed, sounding bored. "Do we just pencil it in on the rounds log?"

"Yeah, we'll have to. Day shift really needs to tighten up their paperwork. I'll have a word with Sam about it before I leave, for all the good that will do. The man is incredible when it comes to what he's accomplished here, but he's more disorganized than a car full of cats."

"G'night, Snotty." Footsteps moved closer, and Penny's view disappeared again. "You good in there, mate? Lucy says you should be good to go in a couple of days." Jeff paused. "Lucy, is the bunyip bigger than it was yesterday?"

More footsteps. Penny was jostled to the back of the cage. "Nah. He just likes to wriggle around. Are we done?"

The footsteps moved away, and a door clicked open, then shut. The ephemeral body surrounding Penny shrank back and nudged her. Unbalanced, she toppled forward against the cage door, expecting to crash against it. Instead, it opened, and Penny tumbled onto the floor.

The cage snapped shut and the creature inside—*the bunyip*, Penny thought with a shudder—hunched back into a corner.

"Red?" Penny called in a loud whisper.

One of the cage doors rattled. Penny raced over to find Red sitting inside, awkwardly hunched over in the tiny space.

The door was locked, and Penny had no idea where the key was. "I'm gonna have to break it somehow. Sit tight."

Red whimpered, but Boots hissed at the bunyip's cage again.

"Uhh, Red? Don't freak out, okay?" Penny's stomach muscles clenched as she tried not to react to the bunyip's arm as it reached out between the cage bars. It was far too long and had too many elbows. Still, it did the trick. It clawed at the lock on Red's cage and popped it open a moment later. As the bony arm disappeared, Penny mustered up a weak but grateful, "Thank you."

Red exploded from the cage in a puff of fur, frizzed with static from the metal. He licked Penny's cheek and she giggled, then made for the exit.

"Are they gone?" she asked.

They made it out of the building safely, though with a few extra scrapes thanks to the wonky vent grate. Penny wriggled through the fence gap first, then waited for Red.

Halfway through, he froze. Then, whimpering, he frantically pushed through. Sensing his urgency, Penny grabbed his front paws and yanked him free. Just as Red rolled under the electric fence tape, his body contorted.

The fence snapped loudly, and the scent of burnt fur wafted past.

Red hustled to his feet, limping. He ignored Penny's questions and headed straight for a tree. When Penny followed, he bared his teeth until she backed away. The rainforest darkened as the moon slid behind a cloud.

Several moments later, Red emerged from behind the tree, stark naked and in human form. "Sorry for growling at you, Penny."

"Don't be sorry for snapping, be sorry for flashing." Penny spun, turning her back on him to avoid the sight of him cupping his manhood with his cheeks as red as his hair.

"Ah, fuck! Sorry, lass."

"You want me to go find your clothes?" Penny offered.

"Nah. It's dark. I'll make a run for it." Penny waited but didn't hear him move away. "Can we maybe leave this bit *out* of Agent Crenel's report?"

Laughing, Penny made an offer. "I'll give you a two-minute head start. If I see your pasty ass before I get back to my room, it's going in."

She had barely finished talking before twigs snapped and leaves swooshed behind her. When she turned back around, he was nowhere to be seen.

CHAPTER FIFTEEN

The next day's tour began with a drunken party of rabbits.

The Centzon Totochtin were a group that sprang from Aztec culture. Penny wasn't sure how they had made it to Australia. Smuggling the four hundred tiny gods across the world seemed impossible, but the deities didn't act like they were being held against their will.

One rabbit bounded up to Penny and sniffed her knee. Another approached Marge and slipped a tiny paw into her hand, pulling her away from Gerald, who had knelt on the ground to chat with one of the furry Aztec gods.

"Whiskey?" Gerald sniffed a thimble-sized glass. "Yep, smells like whiskey." He took a sip and smacked his lips. "Bloody ripper! That tastes great! You got any more, little matey?"

Marge nervously joined a circle of dancing rabbits. When one pushed her into the middle, she did the only dance she knew—the Nutbush. When the rabbits joined in, tapping tiny feet and kicking them up in time to a beat produced by their stomping, Gerald finally realized what his wife was doing.

"Hey! Let me try!" He jumped to his feet and stuck out two hands, Macarena-style. When he started swaying his hips, humming the tune, half the rabbits flocked toward him.

The two groups faced off in a dance fight that Penny was sure was hilarious, only she couldn't see past the tears of laughter streaming down her face.

When the Centzon Totochtin finally dispersed, Penny's stomach hurt from all the laughter. She quickly sobered, though, when Sam announced the next stop.

"We have a real live bunyip in our rehab facility." He waited for the gasps and excitement to calm down. "I know, a real Aussie legend, right? Now, we can't let you pet it—" There was a smattering of laughter at that. "But we're going to let you watch feeding time."

"You're going to feed it a *human?*" Whoever shouted the question from the crowd had echoed Penny's thoughts.

Surely, he wouldn't.

"Not a *real* human," Sam reassured the watching crowd. "It's a pig. We've just…dressed it up a bit."

"The bloody bunyip's getting a better breakfast than I did," Gerald muttered. "Fancy giving a nice fat slab of bacon to the attraction and not your guests?"

To Penny's surprise, Sam led the group away from the wildlife hospital and over to a large, glass-fronted enclosure. A rope barrier kept the spectators several feet back, despite it being low enough to step over.

Inside, stunted gum trees drooped over a shallow pond.

The clear water stirred, and a trail of bubbles moved toward the bank, then receded.

A hatch snapped open at one side. A body shot out, towed by a rope that stretched from one side of the compound to the other. *Not a body*, Penny realized. *A pig.*

The pig wore a blue sundress, a wide-brimmed hat, and a pair of oversized sunglasses. Crooked lipstick was smeared on its bristly mouth, and gloves covered the two front trotters. A blue sneaker dragged along the ground, the other shoe lost somewhere in the leaves.

"See?" Gerald grumbled. "They could have sliced her up for the barbeque. Bacon in a dress is still bacon!"

If Sam heard the complaint, he didn't show it. Instead, he leaned over, making the rope barrier lean toward the glass. "Come on, B. You need to eat, buddy."

He spoke softly, not to his audience, but to the bunyip, coaxing it out with the concern of a man imploring his sick dog to eat.

The bunyip exploded out of the water, triple-jointed arms stretching out from a shapeless, shadowy mass before they darted down to skewer the pig-woman. The tourists squealed in fear and delight. Claws ripped through the tough pig flesh, shoveling it past a wide, hinged jaw, dress and all. Seconds later, the bunyip receded as quickly as it had appeared, still chewing the enormous meal.

Penny got up on her tiptoes, craning her neck. "Where did it go?" she asked Red, who stood beside her, a good foot taller.

"It's still in there," he said. "I can see the shadow moving. Dunno how. That water isn't deep enough for a fat beastie like that."

Penny turned to him. "Red, how did they get it over here? We're half a klick from the—"

Red gave a quick shake of his head, his eyes slipping toward Sam. The owner of the Flying Crow still faced glass, but his body had stilled.

Penny snapped her mouth shut.

"I know, right?" Amelia lifted her insulated coffee cup. "Who'd have thought it would stay hot?"

Despite being grateful for the rescue, Penny eyed Amelia warily. "I still can't believe you brought coffee with you. In this heat?"

Amelia shrugged and took another sip. "Hot and tired, or hot and caffeinated? I'm starting to regret making fun of how cold you get back in Portland."

The tour ended soon after that with an abruptness that made Penny uneasy. Back in the tent, she asked Amelia if she felt the same.

"I didn't notice anything weird." Amelia absentmindedly scratched Boots on the head. "You're probably just paranoid, Penny. No wonder. From what Red said, you guys were half a second away from being busted. Crenel would kick your ass if he knew that."

"Well, he's not going to find out from me," Penny pointed out. Still, she winced when the agent in question texted her, asking her to meet with him as soon as she had a free moment.

Rather than drag it out, Penny messaged him back.

Right now. Your place or mine?

I'll come to you.

Crenel must've expected her response because the tent zip opened moments later. Crenel ducked through and closed behind him before casually taking a seat at the end of Penny's bed. "Progress report."

"I went looking for information last night," Penny admitted. "I found the holding center where they house and treat injured Mythers. They had a few unusual residents, but nothing I can categorically say shouldn't be there." She handed her phone to Agent Crenel, already open at the pictures she had taken. "It does look like they're treating them."

"What about the bunyip?" Crenel pressed. "Red told me you saw it in there. Was it properly restrained? A cannibalistic creature like that could wreak all kinds of havoc if it got out."

"Well, I wouldn't say it was restrained." Penny explained the ease with which the bunyip had broken out of its cage and its surprising behavior. "It seemed as if it could get out at any time. I don't know what they're treating it for, but maybe it's biding its time until it's well?" Penny shrugged, at a loss.

Crenel didn't look satisfied with her answer. "That doesn't sound safe. Still, if all we have to bust this guy on is an OHS violation, it will have to do."

He stood to go. Penny reached out a hand to stop him, then pulled back.

"What is it, kid?" When Penny didn't answer, Crenel folded his arms and frowned. "You think we've got the wrong guy, don't you?"

"I didn't say that," Penny protested. "But...maybe we do?

And maybe, even if we don't, it's not what we think it is. We don't have any evidence that this guy smuggles, trades, or even *looks* at the Mythers funny."

"So, you want to wait until we get more evidence." It was quite clearly a statement, not a question. Crenel ran a frustrated hand through his hair. "We're going to run out of time. If you don't want this guy busted, we need to clear his name. How are you going to do that?"

Penny threw her hands in the air, frustrated. "I don't know! We don't have the authority to run this as a full operation. We're hamstrung."

Crenel opened his mouth to respond, then looked down at the colorful serpent insistently head-butting his knee. "What is it, Boots? Are you volunteering to help us?"

Boots nodded eagerly.

"No. No way!" Penny shook her head, then pointed a warning finger at Amelia, who looked for all the world like she was about to agree with a snake. "I said I had doubts. That's the exact *opposite* of being certain. What if I'm wrong? What if something goes wrong, and Boots gets hurt?"

"Boots, did you speak to the bunyip?" Crenel asked.

Boots nodded.

"Do you think this is risky?" He continued.

The serpent shook her head.

"You're taking the word of someone who can't even talk," Penny pointed out.

Amelia walked over and took a seat beside Penny. "Penny, you kind of did that when you brought Boots to America. I know, I know. You couldn't have stopped her if you wanted to, and this is no different. Do you really think she's going to let you leave her home?"

Penny stood and moved away from her friend. "This is completely different! She snuck into my suitcase! What was I supposed to do, abandon her at the airport?"

Boots coiled around a bedpost, shinnied up it, and shot along the top railing. She wrapped her tail around it, then dropped her head so it was level with Penny's. Boots launched into a barrage of hissing, occasionally pausing and shaking her head as if she simply couldn't believe the stupidity she was hearing. She ended with a hiss, a cough, and a solid head-butt to Penny's nose. Then, she released her grip and dropped onto the floor. Boots slithered over to sit next to Agent Crenel, who had a hand covering what was *clearly* a smirk, and waited patiently for Penny's response.

For a moment, Penny was too shocked to respond. Eventually, she sighed. "Fine. Traitor. I'm not even going to lecture you about how I was only doing this for your own good."

Crenel reached out a surreptitious hand, and Boots slapped the palm with her tail.

"Great." Penny grabbed her pillow, bunching it into a ball. "You've taught my snake to high-five. She doesn't *have* five; she doesn't even have one. Get out of here, old man. You're a terrible influence."

"I'll come back in an hour to hear your amazing plan." Crenel slipped out of the tent just in time to avoid the pillow tossed at his head, although Penny could swear she heard him chuckle as he walked away.

"Bastard."

CHAPTER SIXTEEN

The plan, in the end, was simple. Approach Sam, offer him a once-in-a-lifetime deal with Boots as the bait, and arrest him as soon as the money changed hands. "Simple," Penny repeated to herself, wiping her sweaty palms on her jeans.

Twenty feet away, Sam was deep in conversation with Sophie. Penny hovered behind some clumping bamboo, waiting for the perfect moment to approach the refuge owner. "Just set up an illicit deal with the dangerous smuggler. No big. It's not like he could possibly suspect I'm up to anything, right?"

Sam finished his conversation, then looked directly at Penny. He waved goodbye to his companion and headed toward her.

Penny plastered a bright smile on her face and stepped out to meet him. "Hi, Sam!"

"Hi." He crossed his arms and waited for her to speak.

He's not making this easy on me, Penny thought. *I'm just gonna have to go for it.*

"You have an amazing assortment of Mythers here, Sam. Where do you get them all?" She cringed internally at the obviousness of her question.

"Here and there," Sam said. Just when Penny thought he wouldn't volunteer any more information, he continued. "Most of them are rescues. Creatures that we found injured or ill. Some were relocated because their natural environment was under threat—usually some big, fancy development going in. And, a few *want* to come to us. We've got quite the reputation in the Myther community."

"Wow." Penny bit her lip, her gut twisting uneasily. Something about this felt wrong. *I can't back out now. If he's innocent, this will go at least a little way to clearing his name.* "I'm surprised to see you only have the one rainbow serpent. There are over a dozen in the country now."

Sam's expression softened a little. "I've seen a few in my time. Beautiful creatures."

"I, um, know where you can get one." Penny didn't give herself any space to back out. "A bigger one, and a bit smarter than the one you have now. I have one. She is for sale. I could —"

"No." Sam's face hardened, and he turned on his heel.

"It's a one-time offer." Penny didn't have time for games. She didn't want him to take the deal, but she had to be sure. "Ten grand. I've got her here with me, hidden away. No one knows I have her. She's untraceable."

Sam froze. He slowly turned back to look at her. "Do you know what the fines are if you're caught selling a Myther? There's a good chance of jail time, too."

Penny swallowed, disappointment quickly hardening

into fury. *I will take you down, you son of a bitch.* "That's only if you get caught. There's paperwork to take care of, but…"

The muscle in Sam's jaw worked for a moment while he considered her offer. "I know a guy who can do the papers. Ten thousand, not a cent more. I'd recommend against approaching random people next time you want to do something this illegal, though." He glanced around. "This isn't the time or the place to discuss this. We'll meet tonight."

Penny nodded, her heart racing a million miles an hour as Sam gave her directions to an unused holding bay at the back of the refuge. "Come alone. Bring the snake." This time, he left without looking back. As soon as he was out of sight, she fired off a text message to Agent Crenel.

He took the bait. The handover is tonight. Is there any chance of calling in backup for this one?

His reply didn't give her any security.

I'm working on it now.

Penny skipped dinner, the bundle of nerves in her gut too tight to allow her to eat anything. She insisted Amelia attend and take Red and Cisco with her. "I don't want him to think anything is up. He won't be too surprised if I'm not there, but if we're all absent, he might get worried."

Agent Crenel waited behind with Penny. He paced in her tent, his frustration growing by the minute. "This whole situation is a mess of barely-there information. They *think* a local team is nearby, and they *think* they'll be able to attend. Why the hell can't I talk to them myself?"

"Can you calm down? You're making me nervous." Penny fidgeted with Boots' tail. The serpent butted her hand with irritation. "Sorry, Boots. Blame Crenel."

Boots tossed her head dismissively.

Crenel came to an abrupt halt, turning to face Penny and Boots. "If you want to call this off, we can. We don't know if Sam is working alone. For all we know, half the staff here is in on this operation. If backup falls through, it'll be the just five of us against who knows how many people. We don't know if they have weapons, backup, or an escape plan." Boots hissed at Agent Crenel, and he quickly corrected himself. "Six of us. Regardless, going it alone is a terrible idea."

"This whole thing was your idea," Penny reminded him. "We can't back down now. That bastard almost fooled me into trusting him! I can't let him get away with trafficking someone like Boots. If I bail now, Sam will know something is up. We might not get another chance."

"And if you lose Boots?" Crenel dropped his cigarette just outside the tent, stepping out to grind it into the ground.

"You know I won't let that happen." Penny's hand reflexively tightened around her friend. "Not ever."

The conversation continued to go in circles, Crenel cursing the FBI and their Australian contacts and insisting Penny drop the case, and Penny refusing. She *had* to see this through.

"You're right." Crenel pulled out another cigarette and lit it. "We can't back out. It's too late, and we won't get another chance."

"That's exactly what I've been saying for the last two

and a half hours. It's not like you to agree with me, Agent Crenel." Penny narrowed her eyes, suspicion blossoming. "Did you just try to reverse-psychology me?"

"Damn. It didn't work." Crenel dodged the rolled-up sock Penny pegged at his head. "Look, I don't like waiting, okay? My nerves aren't what they used to be. This desk job has made me soft."

"It's not the desk job that made you soft, Agent." Penny's grin was triumphant. "You just don't want to admit you give a damn about us. You've come to care for us meddling kids."

"Never!" Crenel barked. His eyes, however, held a twinkle of mirth.

Finally, Amelia returned to the room with Red and Cisco. It was quickly established that all three were on board to continue with the mission, even in the absence of any official backup from the FBI or any of the local agencies. Crenel's contact had assured them a team was already there and in place, but the total radio silence from their supposed allies suggested otherwise.

"Red will wait here. Amelia here, Cisco there, and I'll keep watch from there." Crenel's finger stabbed various places on the crude tourist map. "Is your audio set up and ready to go?"

"Aye, aye, Captain." Red saluted the agent, and Penny lifted her shirt so Crenel could examine the wire taped to her torso.

Crenel nodded approval. "Not bad, not bad. Cisco, how are you doing over there?"

"We're not exactly armed for a firefight, but I think it'll do." Cisco pointed at four sets of various weapons laid out on one of the beds. "I've given Penny the small basic kit in case she needs to get out of a bind. Pliers, lock picks, scissors, rope—you know, the usual things. In addition, she has a garrote, two knives, and a Glock. Red is farthest away, so he'll get —"

Crenel held up a hand for silence while he answered his phone. "What do you mean, they're here? We haven't heard a goddamn peep from them. I'm trying to run a complicated operation here. No, that's not good enough. I've got four kids running a bust on an international smuggling ring, and their backup is nowhere to be seen. Does that sound okay to you? No, they're in their twenties." Crenel squinted at Penny. "They look like kids to me. Look, just make it happen. The last thing we need is a team of Australian feds crashing our sting."

He stabbed his phone screen to end the call, looking like he'd rather slam it down instead. "The office keeps trying to tell me there's already a local team here. They're in the area and they know where we are, but they're dark. We can't count on them for backup. Last chance to back out, kids."

"No way, Grandpa." Penny winked at Boots, who chuckled. "Are we ready, Princess?"

Boots bounced her head up and down, then slithered over to the bed. She lifted her head and nosed the handgun.

Cisco snatched it out of her reach when she tried to pick it up. "No, Boots!" he scolded. "That is not cool. You don't get to handle one of those until you've been trained how to use it."

Boots hissed angrily, then chuckled again.

"She's having way too much fun," Amelia pointed out.

"If we're not careful, our next operation will be led by the snake."

"Behave, you." Penny lifted a warning finger at Boots. "I'm serious. If you give me any reason to think you're not going into this with a suitable level of caution, you will stay here. I don't care if I have to go into this trade with a rubber snake from the gift shop."

Once Boots looked suitably chastened, Penny began to secret the weapons away. She tucked the gun in the back of her waistband, slid a knife down her boot, and strapped another to her forearm.

"You're gonna look strange going out with long sleeves in this heat," Crenel pointed out.

Penny shook her head. "Have you seen the size of the mosquitoes out there? Any Australian worth their salt knows that a bit of sweaty humidity is no match for a horde of bloodsucking monsters."

Soon, there was nothing left to prepare. The minutes ticked by, and finally, it was time.

Penny crouched in front of Boots and held out a small glass bottle. It had once held whiskey and was now filled with sparkling clean water. "In you go."

Boots lifted up and flickered her tongue at Penny's cheek. Then she dove, her body twisting and narrowing as it slipped into the tiny bottle. Penny screwed the cap on and then held it up to the light. "You're so tiny!" She tapped the side of the bottle. Boots gave a dramatic wiggle and buried her head amongst the coils of her body.

Penny tucked the bottle into her back pocket. "Let's do this." She touched each of her weapons, ensuring each one was secure, then stepped out of the tent. "Give me a ten-minute head start," she said. Sam would likely have eyes on her as she arrived at the meeting place, and she didn't want to risk the others being seen.

Penny jogged through the compound, the minor exertion beading her forehead with sweat. The metal of the gun had been cool when she first slipped against her skin, but it was now warm. *I wonder how much you have to sweat to disable a weapon?*

She slowed as she approached the meeting place, her senses alert, and the hair on the back of her neck prickling with anticipation.

Sam waited for her outside a small brick building. The white paint was old and flaking, and the light that shone through the barred window flickered yellow. Penny swallowed hard and walked up to him, mindful of the crunch of gravel under her feet.

"Did you bring the serpent?" Sam asked, his voice cold.

The hardness in his face was enough to make Penny take a step back. She glanced around, suddenly aware that their meeting place was surrounded by thick rainforest. Of course, she had known that from her reconnaissance beforehand. Now, she could only hope her friends were the only ones hiding in it.

She held up the small bottle and nodded. Sam reached out, but she snatched it back. "Did you bring the cash?" Penny knew an arrest wouldn't stick without the exchange.

Sam smirked. "You don't accept bank transfer?"

Penny shook her head firmly. Any smuggler worth his salt would know that a transaction like this would be cash only. True to her suspicions, Sam nodded at a suitcase propped up against the building.

"Open it." Penny cursed the high pitch of her voice. It wouldn't do to show this scum how nervous she was.

Sam regarded her for a moment, then nodded. He sauntered over to the suitcase and picked it up. When he walked back to her, he balanced it on one hand and snapped open the clips. He drew out two fat envelopes. "You want me to open them for you, too?"

Penny nodded.

Sam slipped a finger under the envelope flap and pulled it open. Before he showed her the contents, he nodded at the jar. "She's a bit small. You told me she was bigger than the one we already have."

Penny pursed her lips and unscrewed the lid. Boots slithered out, taking the opportunity to play up the startling shift into a full-sized serpent. She coiled her body into loops, sitting patiently next to Penny.

"You're not worried she'll run away?" Sam asked, holding the envelopes full of cash in a white-knuckle grip.

"She'll do what I tell her. The money?" Penny clamped down on her impatience. She couldn't risk this deal going sideways, as much as she wanted it over and done with.

Sam thumbed the envelope open and showed her. Penny nodded at the neatly stacked fifty dollar notes inside. When he showed her the second wad of money, her stomach unclenched a little. They were almost done.

"Back in the jar, snake." Penny held out the bottle, and Boots obediently slunk into it. This time, Penny made sure the lid was only screwed on loosely. If something went wrong, she wanted to be sure Boots would be able to get it off.

Penny held out the jar. Sam held out the money. Penny

grabbed the envelopes, tugging them out of his grip as she reluctantly let go of her friend. It was done.

Chaos erupted. Bright light flooded the area and a dozen people stepped out of the trees, their bodies cloaked in heavily padded vests and tactical helmets. "Get down, get down! On the ground!"

Crenel's backup. The thought flashed through Penny's mind just as something hard slammed between her shoulder blades, throwing her onto the ground. "In the trees! We've got company. Freeze!"

Penny sucked a breath into her stunned lungs. "Boots!" She screamed again as her hands were yanked behind her back and cold metal bit into her wrists as she was handcuffed.

"She's armed!" a voice bellowed in her ear. "You're under arrest. Don't even think about trying to buy your way out of this one, you scumbag poacher."

It took Penny a moment to realize the voice was talking to her. "What? *I'm* under arrest?"

Somewhere to her left, she could hear a muffled yell. "FBI! FBI, stand down, you sons of bitches!"

"FBI? You got no jurisdiction here, arsehole. Who the fuck are you, anyway?" It felt like the whole clearing paused, waiting with bated breath as the leader of the Australian team stormed toward Crenel. "Jesus Christ. Stand down."

Penny's hands were jerked up again, and the handcuffs fell away. The officer who yanked her to her feet was less than gentle, and Penny had to resist snapping at him. She whirled around, spotting Sam in the chaos. "Where the fuck is Boots? What the hell is going on?"

"Who the hell is Boots?" The confusion on Sam's face shifted to realization, and he drew out the jar. He looked at Penny, looked at the shrunken snake, and unscrewed the lid. "Come on, beautiful. Looks like you've been the subject of a major misunderstanding tonight."

Boots erupted from the jar, landing at Sam's feet with a splash. She shot toward Penny and examined her for injury, prodding at Penny's wrists with her nose.

"It's okay, love." Penny kept her voice low. "Just a little bruised."

Crenel stormed over to a man with a phone against his ear. "You want to tell me why the fuck you arrested my people instead of our perp?"

"*Your* people?" The federal policeman interrupted his phone call, his voice rising with incredulity. "We didn't even know you were here. Sam called this in because he was offered smuggled goods. You've got no goddamn business setting up a sting here without going through the proper channels. You almost got your people shot."

"Proper channels?" Crenel seethed. "I've been on the phone trying to pull resources for this all day. It was *your* department that told us to go ahead and promised their team in the area was informed and present."

The officer gaped, shook his head, and turned his back on the agent. A minute later, he wheeled around and yelled into his phone. "What do you fucking mean, you knew this was going down? No, I'm on a fucking job, I didn't check my goddamn emails. I'm working, not on a goddamn holiday."

"Is your wrist okay?" Sam asked Penny.

She realized she had been rubbing it. "Just a little

bruised. When those guys take someone down, they mean it."

Sam hesitated, then held his hand out. Penny let him examine the damage.

"It's bruised, with some skin abrasion." He let it go. "You're really with the FBI?" Penny nodded, and he screwed his face up in confusion. "Then what's all this? Why set me up if you came to help?"

It was Penny's turn to feel confused. "Help? We thought you were running a smuggling ring. We came to bust you, not help."

Sam's shoulders slumped, and a look of defeat passed over his face. "I should have known. It's because of my family ties, isn't it?"

Penny didn't see any reason to hide the truth from him. "You're Silas, aren't you? Silas Nevins."

Sam hesitated, then nodded. "I haven't gone by that name for a long time, but yeah. That's me."

"What's going on?" Penny asked him. "I mean, if you pulled in the feds because you thought a smuggling deal was going down, I'm guessing you're not smuggling anything yourself. Right? But if they're on your side, why do you need the FBI's help?"

"Someone has been stealing our animals." Sam bit out the words, an undercurrent of anger flowing through each one. "At least, that's what it started with. We lost a couple of rare birds, a dingo, and an old Bengal tiger we had rescued from a circus down in Tassie, so we got some Mythers in. Some are more sentient than others. They agreed to hang around and keep an eye on things. They turned out to be a bigger draw than the native animals, and as much as I hate to say it, we need the funding the tourists bring in to keep going."

"So you converted your animal sanctuary into a refuge for hunted Mythers?" Penny's respect for the man was growing by the minute. "And then your thief started targeting *them*."

Sam nodded. "I tried to get the feds involved the first time, but they couldn't help. I mean, we don't keep anything in captivity here. All the Mythers are free to come and go as they wish."

"How do you know they were stolen, then?" Penny asked.

Sam blew out a slow breath. "I just…*know*. Crazy, right? But when a Myther shows up at the same time of day, every day, for months, then suddenly vanishes?" He crossed his arms and looked at the ground. "The feds and I have a pretty good relationship. They told me to file a police report each time it happened, but unless I could show some kind of proof…"

"Do you even *have* local cops out here?" Penny asked in disbelief.

Shaking his head, Sam told her that technically they were under the jurisdiction of the nearest town. "They came out and took a report. When I say 'they,' I mean 'he.' One cop. One guy working every crime in a one-hundred-klick radius. What was he gonna do?"

Penny bit her lip. "You don't think… I mean, your family?"

"That they're the ones stealing from me?" Sam gave a sardonic chuckle. "It wouldn't surprise me, the bastards. I haven't been in contact with them for years, though. I'm not even sure if they know where I am these days."

"What are you going to do now?" Penny fought the urge to offer her assistance. She might have the credentials—or she would when she graduated—but not the jurisdiction.

Sam mustered up a brave smile. "I'll figure it out. Maybe now that the AFP are here, they'll offer a helping hand."

"I'll do what I can to make sure that happens." Penny put her hand out to shake Sam's. "I'm sorry for thinking you were a dirty poacher."

"And I'm sorry for thinking you were a filthy smuggler." Sam grinned. "You know, the outback experience officially ends tomorrow morning. The staff doesn't ship out until the following day, though. If you wanted to hang around, I could offer you a behind-the-scenes tour?"

"That's a definite yes." Penny looked over to where Agent Crenel and the Australian federal officer were still griping over the lack of communication between the organizations. "I don't think I'm gonna get to go to bed anytime soon, though. I don't suppose there's a coffee bar that's still open?"

CHAPTER SEVENTEEN

As Penny had anticipated, her head didn't touch her pillow until daybreak. Her alarm blared an hour later and she sat up, rubbing her eyes.

"Go away." Amelia flung a pillow at Penny's phone but missed it. "Go *away!*"

"If I have to get up, so do you." Penny tossed Amelia's pillow back to her. "Debriefing is in twenty minutes."

"That was Crenel's idea, wasn't it? I never realized dinosaurs don't need sleep to survive." Despite her protests, Amelia rolled out of bed. She looked down at her rumpled clothes. "That'll do. If he wants me to look nice, he can let me have at least three hours of sleep."

"Have you ever known Crenel to complain that someone was underdressed?" Penny swung her legs off her bed, dropping her feet straight into her unlaced boots. "He won't even notice that we are still wearing yesterday's clothes."

Amelia stretched and yawned. "It's a shame we couldn't

stay longer and help Sam. Surely there's something we can do?"

Penny shrugged. The same thought had weighed on her all night. "Maybe we can. It would mean we will miss our final exams, though. Do you think Dean March would give us an extension?"

Amelia slapped a palm against her forehead. "I can't believe I forgot about those. I haven't cracked a textbook since the train ride. I'm not ready!"

"All the more reason to ask if we can stay." Penny hoisted herself to her feet. "But I'm not doing a damn thing until I've eaten. I think staying up all night screwed with my metabolism. I am starving!"

The debriefing session was held in the dining room, much to Penny's joy. Agent Crenel talked while she tucked into a plateful of fake bacon, baked beans, mushrooms, and sourdough toast.

"We're still not sure where the breakdown in communication occurred, but at the very least, our documentation is in place." Crenel shuffled some papers. "We are still trying to reconcile the tip-off that we got that Nevins, the other Nevins, was in this area. At this point, it looks like it was false information, someone getting Geoffrey mixed up with his brother. I want to track down the source, though. Sam's been having some trouble, and I want to make sure Geoffrey isn't the cause of it."

Penny nearly choked on her excitement. "So, we can stay and investigate the missing Mythers?"

Crenel shook his head. "No. We'll have to do the legwork from back home. The AFP isn't best pleased with us at the moment." He waved down the protest Penny made around her mouthful of food. "I know, I know. It wasn't our fault. That doesn't make it any easier for them to swallow."

"Are we sure they'll follow this up?" Penny asked. "Crenel, we can't just leave Sam to deal with this on his own."

Crenel hurried to reassure her. "Agent Davies assures me that they'll be back in a few days to complete a thorough investigation. He'll need to clear it with his superiors, but from the sound of it, they're just as embarrassed about the debacle last night as we are. He is confident they will approve the manpower and resources he'll need to get to the bottom of this."

Penny sat back, mollified. The missing Mythers would be dealt with, and her stomach was full. "Does Sam know yet? Can we tell him?"

"On the record? No." Crenel didn't elaborate, but Penny took it to mean that she could give the refuge owner a quiet heads-up.

Penny licked sauce off a finger. "Are we leaving with the tourists, or can we stay? Sam invited us to stick around for an extra day."

"We can stay," Crenel said. "I haven't booked our flights back yet, so we'll need to grab a hotel for a night or two anyway."

"Please tell me we aren't flying coach." Red stretched. "Mack will send us a plane, right?"

"Assuming the jet's available," Crenel confirmed. "But it won't arrive in an instant. I'll contact Mack today and ask."

"What do we do until then?" Penny asked. "Do we just have to wait for the AFP to get their shit together?"

"Pretty much." Crenel shuffled his papers into a pile and stood. "Enjoy your breakfast. Take a tour. Relax, and try to stay out of trouble for once, okay?"

Penny shoved a forkful of fried mushrooms into her mouth and saluted. "Mmmhmm."

"Damn," Red muttered. When Cisco asked what was wrong, the Irishman stared forlornly at Penny's plate. "She didn't leave any leftovers."

The tourists left the resort in a flurry of gushing praise and frantic searches for luggage. Penny hugged her parents goodbye and promised to call more often.

"Mum, I'll be home for a visit in six months. A long one, I promise!" Penny endured another hug. "Dad? Help. She's suffocating me."

"And what do you think she'll do to *me* if I get in the way?" Gerald pointed out. "See ya, Penny, my love. Stay safe, and make sure you keep that boy of yours on his toes. You know what I'll do to him if he—"

"Ugh, Dad!" Penny smiled and kissed his cheek. "It's good to know you'll never change. Love you both, now go. Go! You'll miss the next part of your trip."

Marge fussed at Penny again, but Gerald gently steered her toward the train. "She's right, Marge. You don't want to miss the cruise, do you?"

"Gerald, don't be ridiculous. They won't leave without us!" Marge jumped as the train honked loudly. "Oh, cripes. We're the last ones to board. Hurry, Gerald! You're making them wait!"

Gerald obeyed, but not without a sneaky eye roll behind his wife's back. Penny laughed, waving. She stayed on the platform until the train began to roll away.

Back inside, the resort held the empty feeling of a holiday that had ended. Staff bustled around, wheeling trolleys stacked with trash bags and cleaning equipment. Not wanting to get in the way, Penny headed back to her room.

Amelia was napping on the bed, snoring lightly. Boots was stretched out beside her, her head stuffed under a pillow in her favorite sleeping position. Penny sat and pulled her boots off, ready to pass out, but her phone buzzed.

The swagman's ghost is due in twenty. Do you want to meet him in person?

"Hell, yes," Penny muttered. She prodded Boots.

The serpent flicked her tail, and Penny poked her again.

"You wanna come to meet a ghost?" Penny whispered. "Or are you going to stay cooped up in here the whole time?" Although Boots hadn't complained, Penny figured she must be itching to get out and see the rest of the resort.

Her theory was confirmed when Boots yanked her head out from the pillow and gave an enthusiastic nod.

"Come on." Penny slipped her boots back on and headed out. She almost bumped into Cisco.

"Hey, I was just coming to find you. Did your parents get off okay?"

"Yeah. Mum was a bit teary, but she'll have forgotten that by the time they hit the next leg of their trip."

"The New Zealand cruise, right?" Cisco had suffered through a long conversation with Marge, where she showed him the brochures, itinerary, and the social media pages of the cruise company.

"That's the one." Penny grabbed his hand. "Come see the swagman with me!"

He happily agreed, and they headed out together. Instead of the awkwardly slow shuttle, Sam waited in a four-wheel drive. "Hop in, guys!" He looked around. "Just the two of you?" When Boots gave an offended hiss, he quickly apologized. "The three of you. Sorry, Boots."

"Amelia is sleeping," Penny admitted.

Cisco laughed. "So is Red. Crenel is probably knee-deep in paperwork."

"Off we go, then." Sam flew down the narrow track, taking the corners as though he knew it like the back of his hand.

He probably does, Penny realized. *He lives and breathes this place.*

In truth, she was relieved her suspicions about him had been wrong. Knowing someone was out there looking after the creatures who had crossed the veil but couldn't advocate for themselves—creatures like Boots—was beyond comforting.

They arrived at the billabong just as the sun was heading for its peak over the surrounding trees and touched the water. Penny smelled the swagman before she saw him. The scent of wet leather, old sweat, and strong tea caught her attention as the hummed tune of *Waltzing Matilda* drifted over from the other side of the watering hole.

The swagman stepped out from behind a tree, his melodic notes unwavering as he dropped into a crouch.

Where the jumbuck had come from, Penny had no idea. Though it was just another name for a run-of-the-mill sheep, the Myther creature looked…different. Bigger, woolier, and prouder than the average mutton.

The swagman pounced on the sheep, hollering with glee. "Get that, you fucker! You'll fucking come Waltzing Matilda with me, ya—"

His last word was drowned out by the bleating jumbuck, who bucked and thrashed as it was stuffed into a giant bag.

"I don't remember *that* in the ballad," Penny mused.

Sam chuckled. "Interesting to see what city folk think of the bushies, right?"

"You've picked up our lingo fast," Penny pointed out. "But it still sounds weird with your accent. Do you think you'll settle down here for very long?"

Sam's gaze turned back to the billabong. "It's like I was always meant to be here. I know I'll never be a real Australian, but this is home. I can feel it in my bones."

"Dude, you're the foster parent to a bunyip." Penny socked him lightly in the shoulder. "You're more Aussie than I am!"

They stayed until the swagman, hunted by invisible troopers, screamed a promise that he would never be taken down alive. The ghostly figure threw himself into the still waters of the billabong, with only the gentlest ripple in the water's surface to show that he had ever existed.

"And that's a nursery rhyme they teach you in schools?" Cisco asked with distaste.

"Sure is," Penny confirmed. "Right after the one where

we dance around in circles singing about the plague, and the kid's lullaby about dead babies hanging from trees."

"Point taken." Cisco pulled the land cruiser door shut behind him. "And yet, people wonder why most of the stuff coming through the veil is nasty."

They arrived back at the resort to find three staff anxiously waiting for Sam's return. He killed the engine and climbed out of the car.

"What happened?" He barked.

"The bunyip is gone." Penny immediately recognized the man speaking as Peter. "I swear to God, boss. He was there last night."

"Check the cameras," Sam suggested. "Maybe he just went for a stroll."

Peter hesitated. "The cameras died just after midnight. Boss, all the locks were busted open. B wouldn't do that. If he wanted out, he would have just slipped under the door."

Penny suppressed a shudder at the thought of the monstrous, bony creature contorting itself to slip through the narrow gap beneath the door.

Sam reached into the back of his car, pulled out a shotgun, and walked away.

Penny hurried after him. "Sam! You can't just go around shooting people. Let us help!"

"That bunyip is one of the most valuable creatures we have," Sam called over his shoulder without breaking his stride. "He's a prime target for poachers. If someone has him, they're not gonna let him go just because we asked nicely."

Penny yanked her phone out of her pocket. Crenel picked up after only a single ring, but Penny didn't wait for him to speak. "Whoever is poaching the local Mythers took Sam's bunyip. We are headed over to the wildlife hospital now to check it out. Can you meet us there?"

"Be there in five." Crenel didn't bother to say goodbye before ending the call, but Penny knew he would likely be on the phone to the feds before she'd put her phone back. She could only hope he was able to bring in backup on time.

Whoever had broken into the hospital building hadn't bothered to hide it. "They either know you're onto them, or they don't care anymore." Penny nudged the gate open with her toe, careful to avoid any sections that might contain fingerprint evidence. "How much would a bunyip fetch on the black market anyway?"

"Six figures." Sam stepped through the gate behind her. "With a score like that, I wouldn't be surprised if they packed up and left. I can't let them get away with B!"

"How would they take him against his will?" Penny asked as they entered the small brick building. "When I was in the hospital, he opened his cage like it wasn't even locked."

"An airtight container would stop him from escaping. Theoretically, he doesn't need to breathe. Damned if I know how they'd get him *into* it, though." Sam fell silent for a moment, then grabbed Penny's arm and pulled her around to face him. "Wait a minute. When the hell were you in here?"

Penny shrugged. "I thought you were a dirty poacher, remember? Red and I did some sneaking around the first night we were here. We broke into the hospital through a vent in the ceiling." She grinned at Sam. "I have to say, you take great care of your patients, but you really need to get your shit together when it comes to security."

Peter narrowed his eyes at her. "Three nights ago?"

Penny nodded. "Boots negotiated with the bunyip. I hid in his cage."

Sam opened his mouth to say something, but Peter cut him off. "That's the same night that big shaggy dog went missing." He winced at his boss. "We just assumed you brought him in and forgot the paperwork again. When he was gone in the morning, we figured the same thing, to be honest."

"I…know nothing about a dog. Since when do we take dogs in?" Sam turned to Penny. He folded his arms, slowly tapping one toe as he waited for her explanation.

Penny spread her arms wide. "It's classified. But don't worry, the, uh, *dog* is perfectly fine."

Exasperated, Sam shook his head and moved toward the secure area the bunyip had been taken from. He gingerly pushed the door open, the door handle still attached to the jam. "They really did a number on the place."

"They didn't care about covering their tracks. That's not a good sign. My bet? They either think they're invincible, or they planned to ship out before we saw the damage." Penny peered over his shoulder. It looked like all the cages were still secure except for the big one down the end.

When Crenel arrived, he came with the frustrating news that the AFP wouldn't return until morning. "It's not by choice. They flew out, and their ride has already left. By the time it refuels and gets back to them, it will be daybreak."

"This is bullshit. Every minute we waste increases the chance that we won't catch up with them." Penny thrust her hands into her pockets, resisting the urge to clench her fists in frustration. She watched as Sam paced, growing more frantic by the minute. "Do we at least have permission to help?"

"The Federal Bureau of Investigation absolutely does *not* have permission to interfere with this case." Crenel spoke carefully. "If an *official* member of the Federal Bureau of Investigation were to interfere, it would be a very bad thing."

Penny gave him a small nod, and he turned on his heel and left.

"Well, he's no goddamn help at all," Sam muttered.

Penny smiled brightly. "The hell he wasn't. He just gave us express permission to assist you."

Sam frowned. "I'm pretty sure he just did the exact opposite."

Shaking her head, Penny suppressed a chuckle. She could see the hope brightening on Sam's face despite his skepticism. "*Official* members of the FBI are forbidden to assist. Us? We're students. We're not officially anything."

Relief dawned on Sam's face. "I don't want you getting hurt," he began.

"We won't. We're trained for this." Cisco grinned. "Well, almost trained. We've got a couple of months to go, but we're pretty good at kicking ass and taking names."

With a tight smile, Sam offered a handshake. "Then I'm glad to have you both on my side."

CHAPTER EIGHTEEN

In the end, there was very little Penny could do to help. Despite the blatantly obvious damage to the wildlife hospital, the thieves had left no trace of their whereabouts. Penny pulled in every resource she had, even calling Trevor at the Academy to see if he could get eyes on the area. Unfortunately, the dense Australian bushland worked to their disadvantage.

"Just trees," Trevor insisted. "Trees, trees, a bit of a creek, and some more trees. And ocean—there's a lot of ocean."

Penny growled in frustration. "Fine, but keep watching, and let me know the minute you see something suspicious."

"Sure." There was a muffled voice on Trevor's end. "Dean March says don't forget your exams. You can't put them off forever."

"This is *not* the time," Penny insisted.

"I understand." The Dean's voice came over the phone crystal-clear. "Luckily, a certain Academy liaison submitted paperwork to request a further extension. You have one more week, but I don't think I can push it out further than that."

"Thank you, Dean March." Penny meant it. That extra slice of time would allow her to focus on finding the bunyip, taking on the poachers, and helping Sam. She would just have to do it quickly. "Hey, you haven't seen Bacchus around lately, have you?"

"I have." The Dean sounded amused.

"Can you ask if there's anything he can do to help us down here?" Penny knew it was a long shot, but she had to try.

"I already have." Dean March hesitated, then added, "Bacchus suggested a local deity has taken an interest in the situation. He didn't specify who or what side they are on. For that reason, he was unwilling to get involved."

"Does he have any idea how utterly unhelpful that is?" Penny muttered.

The Dean chuckled. "I have no doubt that he does. You know Bacchus."

"Unfortunately, yes, I do." Penny wished the party god was within arm's reach. "Please tell Trevor I appreciate his help and tell Bacchus he's an asshole. See you when we get back, Dean."

"Of course, Penny. Do take care." Dean March ended the phone call.

Penny let out a deep breath of frustration. "I'm not gonna let that bastard get away with the bunyip. I don't care how long it takes us to track him down, I'm going to find him and kick his ass so hard he tastes leather for a month."

"Penny, there must be something we can do." Amelia

was sitting on her bed, surrounded by the organized chaos of their equipment. She had begun unpacking it an hour earlier, hoping it would inspire an idea or a plan.

"Short of traipsing through the rainforest and hoping we randomly stumble upon their base of operations?" Penny asked. "I can't think of anything. Is Red sure he can't sniff them out?"

Amelia shook her head. "You know how his senses work. They ramp up right before the full moon and dissipate the morning after. He's just a regular hungry guy now."

"Speaking of hungry, it's almost time for dinner." Penny's stomach gave a loud growl. "I feel bad for even thinking about my stomach, but I skipped lunch. Maybe a good feed will shake loose an idea or two."

Amelia looked as immaculate as ever, but Penny insisted on taking a shower before she left for the restaurant. Sam had already warned her that most of the staff had shipped out earlier that day. The menu items consisted of beans on toast or beans without toast, and she would have to wash her own plates afterward. Although Penny had no intention of dressing up, her skin prickled with sweat and grime.

She waved Amelia ahead while she grabbed a clean outfit and headed toward the communal bathroom. She couldn't help but relish the few minutes alone under the dribble of hot water. The water pressure wasn't great, but it was hot enough to unknot her muscles and fill the tiny cubicle with steam. Finally, her skin glowed pink and clean. She stepped out of the shower and quickly dried off.

She dressed, stepped outside, and slapped at a sudden

sting on her neck. As the late afternoon light dimmed and her legs buckled beneath her, she gave a faltering scream.

By the time Penny woke again, all the work she had done loosening her sore muscles had been wasted. Her arms and shoulders screamed in protest at their uncomfortable position, and Penny rolled to her knees with a grunt. Her position was awkward, hindered by tight ropes that bound her hands behind her back and looped around her ankles. Her fingers strained, but couldn't find the knot that would undo them.

She twisted her body, trying to get into a sitting position. Instead, she sprawled on her face. Panic squeezed her chest, pushing her heart up to her throat.

Get it together, girl, Penny told herself. She shook her head, but that only made the muzzy feeling worse. Still, the drugs must be wearing off if she was awake.

Penny took a few slow, deep breaths. "Stay calm. Check your surroundings. Make a plan." The sound of her voice cleared her head a little, and she looked around the tiny room she was being held captive in.

Wherever she was, it was neither the luxurious opulence of the resort nor one of the crumbling old buildings on the property. She kicked her bare foot at the smooth floor, and as she had anticipated, found it hollow. The tiny building was new but cheaply made, and everything Penny could see supported her hunch that she was imprisoned in a fairly new portable building.

Unfortunately, it was empty. Instead of a handle, the

door was held shut by a rather large deadbolt. There was a single window, but heavy metal bars crossed the opening on the inside. Even if she could break the glass, she wouldn't be able to get through the bars. The bare cell held no sharp edges, no protrusions, nothing she could use to help loosen her restraints.

"Guess I'll have to do it on my own, then."

Penny worked at the ropes until her fingernails stung and her skin felt tacky with blood. They didn't budge, but she refused to give up, continuing to claw at her restraints until she heard the rattle of the key in the door. She scurried back into a corner, awkwardly hiding her hands against the wall to obscure the evidence of her failed attempts to escape.

Two men stepped inside, shutting the door behind them. One, she recognized. His features were an echo of Sam's, but harder and crueler.

"Geoffrey Nevins." She stated it as fact.

Nevins didn't seem surprised that she knew him. He smiled at her and beckoned to his friend. "You know who I am, but I don't give a fuck who you are. I don't give a fuck about you at all, except that you've got something I want." He leaned over her, and Penny had to swallow hard to keep the bile in her stomach. "I'm going to ask you some questions. If you answer them, we'll leave. If you don't, I'll leave. Harvey won't. He'll stay until you answer the questions."

Penny spat in his direction. "Who says I'm going to answer anything for you, dipshit?"

Nevins shrugged casually. "I'd rather not have to dispose of your body tonight, but it is what it is. Now, tell me about this magic snake of yours."

Penny refused to answer, then grunted as a hard boot connected with her midsection. She could tell he had held back. She could still breathe, after all.

Nevins asked again, his tone bored. "Tell me about the snake."

"Fuck you." Penny yelped as the boot connected again, this time closer to her kidneys.

"Tell me about the snake." There was a hardness in Nevins's eyes that made Penny's skin crawl.

"What do you want to know?" *I need to buy time.* Penny knew Boots was never far away from her, not when she needed her. Surely, Boots would be leading Penny's friends to her rescue right this moment.

"What is she?" Nevins asked.

Well, that question was easy. Penny had no doubt he knew what Boots was, or he wouldn't have bothered to kidnap her. "She's a Rainbow Serpent. I found her a couple of years back. Is that what you want to know?"

"Does it do what you say?" he pressed.

Have to tread carefully here. "Sometimes," Penny admitted. "But not always. I trained her to stay and to follow me. Sometimes she listens when I say no, and other times, I have to smack her on the nose." Penny knew she would probably get fangs implanted at her nose if Boots could hear her talking this way. She didn't want this brute to know how intelligent her friend was, though.

"Where is she?" Nevins growled the question, and Penny knew that was what he *really* wanted to know.

Penny shrugged. "I don't even know where I am. How the hell am I supposed to know where my pet snake is?"

Two kicks this time, and Penny was left gasping for breath.

"Where is she?"

Penny stayed silent. Another kick, one that made her retch on the floor. She curled into a ball, or tried to, anyway. She braced for the next kick, then flinched at a crash from outside.

"The fuck was that?" The goon looked at his boss. "You want me to keep going here?"

Nevins hesitated. He looked down at Penny, who stared up at him with murder in her eyes. "No, go check it out. We'll come back to this one later. Maybe we'll try something a little more creative on our next attempt."

The goon left. Nevins hesitated at the door and looked back. "You think you're tough, and you might be. Either way, you won't last until morning. You think about that while I'm gone, hey?"

The door slammed shut and the lock clicked. Only then did Penny begin to shake.

Her breath came in shallow gulps, each gasp sending a slice of pain to her ribs. She tried to breathe quietly, straining to hear what was going on outside, but apart from some muffled curses and a vague clatter, she couldn't make anything out. Except—was that thunder? It was, she realized, and rain as well.

I'm stuck on the floor playing weather girl. Is this what my life has come to? As if in response to her unspoken thoughts, someone giggled. It was high-pitched but masculine and sounded out of place among the tough smugglers who loitered outside. The laugh came again, as loud and as clear as though the person were standing right next to her.

Penny yanked her head up to look around. The room was empty, but the shadow of a bird flapping past the window made Penny start, her wrists jerking once more against her bonds.

They vanished.

Penny's wrists and ankles came free with a jerk and she grunted, coming to her feet with a bolt of anxiety. The ropes hadn't just broken, they were *gone.*

"What the fuck?" She briefly considered the possibility that they were magic bonds, designed to release their prisoner if a certain word was spoken or if other conditions were met. She quickly discarded that idea. She knew Nevins did not intend to let her go, not even if she told him what he wanted to know.

Her rush of adrenaline quickly faded when she realized she still couldn't go anywhere. She sat back down on the floor, tucked her knees against her chest, and waited.

Her captors didn't return. Penny's brief glimpse outside had revealed a dark sky, and some kind of compound lit with blinding spotlights. If not for the window and its mottled glass, Penny would be sitting in darkness. *The glass.*

She stood and pushed the window. When that didn't work, she punched it, gently at first to see if it would give, then harder. She was vaguely aware of the patter of raindrops on the roof of her prison cell but ignored it as she pounded on the glass. *If nothing else, this storm might buy me some time.* Her attempts were clumsy, her hands swollen and numb. "Fuck it."

Penny stripped off her shirt, glad she was wearing a crop top underneath, and wrapped it around her elbow.

One solid jab left a star-shaped crack in the window. Another one turned the crack into a spiderweb. Her third attempt almost dislocated her joint, but she punched a hole in the safety glass. Penny picked away the tiny glistening cubes. With some effort and a few sliced fingers, she managed to make a hole a little bigger than her fist. That didn't mean she could escape. The bars were no wider than her arm. It wasn't escape that Penny was after, though.

She poked two fingers through the hole after squeezing a little blood from her torn fingernails and a deep scratch. She felt a raindrop hit her hand, then another. *Patience*, she told herself. After a few minutes, she could feel the rain dribbling off the end of her fingertips.

"Come on, Boots," she whispered fervently. "I know you've got water magic, babe. This is as close to a blood sacrifice as I've got for you. Boots, come and find me."

A smooth, slender thread wriggled up Penny's fingers. She almost jerked her hand back in fright but was glad she had quelled the urge when Boots' head poked through the hole in the window.

Hssss.

Penny kissed the top of Boots' head. "Yes, I know. I was hit with a sleeping dart and trussed up like a Sunday roast. Can you get me out of here?"

The serpent withdrew from the window, and Penny heard a splash as Boots flopped onto the ground. It felt like an age before Boots returned, the clink of keys dragging through the mud behind her. Boots lifted herself up to the window. Penny couldn't see how the serpent had managed to reach the tiny hole, but she was content to write it off as part of the magic her friend possessed.

Penny's elation at her unorthodox rescue was short-lived. Though Boots had returned with a fat keyring full of keys, none of them fit the deadbolt on her door. Key after key, Penny tried them, slipping each one around on the ring to try the next. She ran through the whole ring twice before hurling the whole bunch of them at the wall in frustration.

As the jangling metal thumped against the wall, the door popped open. Penny started, scrambling back in case one of her captors barreled in.

No one did.

"What the hell?" Penny peeked out the door, seeing no one. She looked down at a sniggering Boots. "Was that magic?"

Boots nodded.

"Was it *you?*"

This time, Boots shook her head. The serpent, clearly bored with the line of questioning, slipped out the open door. Penny grabbed the keys and quickly followed, stepping out into the rain and scurrying toward a clump of trees, one arm wrapped around her bruised ribs for support.

Where the hell are we? Penny didn't give that much further thought. They were in Australia, in the rainforest, no less. It was Boots' natural environment, and the serpent likely knew everything about it. Her friend would lead them home, she was sure. "Let's get the bunyip and go."

Penny jogged past a cluster of trees, then stopped to crouch behind a port-a-loo. "Dear God, that smells *awful.* Why are blokes so disgusting?" She eyed a truck at the very edge of the spotlit area, then sorted through the keys until she found one with the same logo printed on the electronic head. "What do you think, Boots? Walk home, or hitch a ride?" The rain intensified. "Ride it is. I'm not risking my life in this downpour. With my luck, we'll be swept away in a flash flood."

She'd driven a rig like that once under controlled conditions in one of Mack's classes at the Academy. It had taken Penny two goes to start it. She would have to hope she could get this monster going before she got caught.

She stepped out from behind the toilet, then darted back as two men passed.

"The bunyip's loaded up, and they're ready to ship out at first light," the first said. "The other one's staying here, though. Nevins wants to broker him personally."

"They've got the werewolf tied up, right?" the second man said. "Otherwise, I'm heading out with the man-eater."

Penny's heart plummeted to her feet. *Red.* It dropped even further when she recognized the second speaker's voice. It was Peter. *Sam will be gutted when he finds out.*

"It's not a full moon, you knob. He can't do squat for another four weeks."

Penny waited until they were gone, then headed back to her temporary jail cell. This time, she noticed two more buildings beside it, tiny prefab constructions designed to be transported in one piece.

"Where's Red?" Penny whispered.

Boots took off, sliding over the wet ground like it was her personal waterslide. Penny hurried to catch up, cringing as cold mud squelched between her bare toes. Halfway to the third building, Penny slipped, landing on her ass in a deep puddle. She cursed and scrambled back to her feet, then over to the shadows between the structures.

She watched for a moment, then, seeing no one, ducked around the corner to free Red.

Key after key refused to fit. She cursed her bad luck. "Dammit! Again? What is it with this place."

Behind her, someone giggled. Penny spun but saw no one, or at least, no humans. A crow flapped down to the ground, stared at Penny, and proceeded to take a shit on the wet dirt.

The incongruity struck Penny, dislodging something at the very edge of her mind. She shook it away as she tried the next key. It didn't fit. She gripped the last key.

The crow wouldn't leave her mind. *Not the crow, the poop.* It hit her in a rush, her brain zapping along a trail of connections.

The out-of-place giggling. Poop-coffee. Bacchus's comment about a deity in the area. Corey and Cora with their raven-black hair. Not *raven*-black. The crow continued to stare at her.

"Wow, what a shame," Penny said aloud, hoping it wouldn't catch the attention of any nearby humans. "If only I could get Red out. Together, we'd cause so much chaos. Oh, well. If this last key doesn't work—" She plunged it into the lock and turned it. She glanced back in time to see the crow launch into the air and flap away. Heart racing, Penny sent up a quick prayer to the heavens. "Thank you, trickster god. Whichever one you are."

Penny pushed open the door and stepped into the makeshift building. Red lay curled up in the corner, the washed-out light slicing through the door highlighting his split lip and black eye. The scent of burning flesh permeated the room.

Penny rushed forward. "Red! What have they done to you?"

Red held out his wrists. A pair of engraved silver manacles cuffed them together, the skin around them raw and blistered. "I think they might know I'm a werewolf."

"Gee, what gave you that idea?" Penny helped him to his feet. "Why did they beat you? Did they think you'd give up Boots?"

"Boots? No, they were trying to make me turn." Red shook his head. "Dumb bastards don't know the first thing about werewolves."

"They figured out you're allergic to silver." Penny quickly examined her keys, but couldn't find anything that looked like it would fit in his cuffs. "Do you think you can put up with that until we get back to the resort?"

"Oh, I wouldn't be so quick to assume you're going anywhere." A shadow filled the doorway, and Penny looked up to see Nevins. He had a gun pointed at her. "I don't know how in the hell you escaped, but I promise we *won't* let it happen again."

Boots darted out from between Penny's legs, angrily hissing at the poacher.

He laughed. "Wonderful. I guess I don't need to keep you around anymore. Unless, of course, you can tell us how to force the change on your big friend here."

Penny spat at him. She didn't bother telling him the obvious—there was no way to force a change on a werewolf. Not the sort Red was, anyway. He would only shift when the moon was full and visible. Penny shifted her posture the tiniest bit, ready to throw herself forward if he so much as flinched. It probably would help, and at least she should die fighting. "Boots, run!"

Boots reared up, then sank her teeth into a fleshy leg. To Penny's horror, she didn't bite Nevins.

Red let out a holler of pain. He snarled, panted, and growled through gritted teeth, "Duck."

Penny threw herself to the ground. Red leapt, his body contorting as it flew through the air, the manacles tumbling to the ground with a clink. The werewolf planted his sharp claws into Nevins's chest and sent him tumbling out the door. Red ducked his head, jaws open, and pressed his teeth to his captor's throat gently enough to avoid bloodshed but not by much.

Penny sprang to her feet. She grabbed the gun that had skidded into a corner and pointed it at Sam's brother. "Well, what do you know? Turns out, there *is* a way to force a change on a reluctant werewolf."

Penny reached one hand behind her back. Boots slapped her tail on it, the reptilian version of a high-five.

"Please!" Nevins begged. "Please, don't let him kill me."

CHAPTER NINETEEN

Penny gratefully accepted the mug of hot chocolate Sam passed her. "And that was when the feds turned up. Poor Red. He shifted back into a human fifteen minutes later. The entire AFP team got to see his bare ass, as pale as the moon. It's just lucky it was overcast. I think the reflection would have blinded us all."

Sam chuckled. "And my brother?"

"They found the bunyip in the truck. That's twenty-five years, at least. By the time you add kidnapping, assault, and the attempted poaching of a human werewolf? You won't be seeing him around here for a while." Penny sipped the warm drink, then reached for a cookie.

Red had retired to his room, icing his bruises and nursing his damaged ego. Amelia, of course, was with him. Crenel had walked out a few minutes ago to take a phone call, and Cisco had followed him at Penny's insistence. She wasn't about to be left in the dark on this one. That left her and Sam alone, chatting quietly about the events that had transpired the night before.

The restaurant doors swung open and Crenel walked back in, tucking his phone into his pocket. "Do you have any idea how hard it is to get a moment's privacy around here?" he demanded, shooting a glare over his shoulder at the trailing Cisco.

"Yup." Cisco winked at the agent. "Damn near impossible."

"What did they say?" Penny asked.

"Nevins' men folded pretty quickly. Turns out, Peter has been working for him from the beginning. Nevins sent him here to apply for the job, along with a couple of other guys who didn't get in. Apparently, Peter developed a conscience over that space of time, and now he wants to confess everything." Crenel scowled. "For a plea bargain, of course. But he's already given us the name of the storage facility that the kidnapped Mythers are being held in. Apparently, none of them have been sold yet. They were waiting to get the bunyip, then planning to smuggle them to Japan to broker the deal over there."

"All of them?" Sam's shoulders slumped in relief. "Thank you, Agent. Thank all of you."

"There's just one last missing piece of the puzzle." Penny turned to Sam. "Did you know you had a trickster god hanging around?"

Sam burst out laughing. "Who, the Crow? Yeah, we named the refuge after him! I originally wanted to call it the 'The Lying Crow,' but the investors didn't like that. The guy—or girl, as it sometimes shows up—is a total pain in the ass. It's been harassing guests here for months. In fact, I heard a rumor that the Crow impersonated one of our staff members and told you our coffee is sourced from owl shit."

"It was bat shit, actually." Penny shook her head. "The trickster god might be a pain in the ass, but he's the only reason we made it out of there alive."

Sam lifted an eyebrow. "I suppose I'll have to go easy on him next time he clogs the toilet."

"How do you tell the difference between a magically-interfered-with toilet and a normal plumbing issue?" Crenel asked, although his face suggested he didn't really want to know the answer to that.

"It's a long drop, Agent Crenel. There is no possible way a giant hole in the ground could clog without the assistance of a trickster god." He watched Crenel's face screw up in horror, then laughed. "Yeah, it was *that* bad."

Crenel pulled out a chair next to Penny. "I just kicked Red out of bed. The AFP will have a team here in twenty, and they've offered us a ride back. After they slam you with questions, of course."

"Great." Penny glanced at Boots. "I can hardly wait."

CHAPTER TWENTY

Penny reclined on her bed in the Academy dorm room she shared with Amelia. "Results are due back today," she said.

Amelia looked up from a half-eaten bar of chocolate. "Yeah, I know. Why do you think I'm stressing so much?"

"I'm sure you did really well. You studied your ass off for those exams!" Penny felt almost guilty. She herself had snuck off on a date with Cisco the night before instead of cramming like her friend.

Still, she knew her subjects and felt like she'd aced the tests. She had to question that confidence, however, when Dean March appeared in the doorway with two large white envelopes embossed with the Academy's seal.

"Girls? I hope I'm not interrupting." Regardless of her hope, the dean entered the room and passed each girl one of the envelopes. "I thought I'd hand-deliver your results."

"That good, or that bad?" Penny asked. She held hers, anxiety welling.

The dean smiled. "Look and see, dear. You might just be surprised at how it all worked out in the end."

"I don't like surprises," Amelia said. She ripped her packet open and scanned the pages inside. "What? I don't get it. What does all this mean?"

"Extra credit," Dean March explained. "For the two field missions you completed this semester."

"But they're applied to *next* semester," Penny pointed out. "Twelve. That's more than…" She stopped, her heart skipping a beat. *It couldn't be! I'm not ready!*

"That's right, Penny." Dean March took a step closer and reached out a hand to shake. "You've already passed your final semester. There is some paperwork to be done, but the two of you—and Cisco and Red, of course—have completed your course in its entirety. Congratulations, girls. You're now fully qualified Mythological Event Specialists."

"No way." Penny's emotions tangled into a ball and tears welled. "We're *done*?"

"As close to it as you can be," the dean confirmed. "But don't worry. We won't kick you out and leave you homeless just yet."

"What the hell do we do next?" Penny's met Amelia's eyes.

Amelia grinned. "We celebrate, of course!"

The celebratory dinner was held the following week. Paddy insisted on hosting, closing the entire bar in honor of the occasion. Penny and the friends she had made over the previous year and a half, both human and mythological, feasted and drank until the wee hours of the morning.

The party was beginning to wind down when Penny collapsed into an empty booth, exhausted from dancing and chatting. Agent Crenel slipped into the seat across from her.

"So," he said, his grin a little sloppy from Bacchus' never-ending supply of wine, "what's next for the golden girl?"

Penny shrugged. "Home. Just for a few weeks. I promised Mum and Dad a family holiday when I graduated. Then I guess I'll come back and fill out the FBI application forms."

Crenel's eyes dropped. "Don't."

"What?" Penny blinked, sure she had misunderstood. "Crenel, that was the whole point, wasn't it?"

"How much harder would it have been to save that bunyip if you'd been a full-fledged agent?" he asked. "Bah. The FBI isn't what it used to be. Too many rules, mountains of paperwork. Things you can avoid if you go out on your own."

"On my own?" Penny sipped her drink, considering. "The FBI has resources I don't," she pointed out.

Crenel nodded. "And Mack and Jessica have resources the government would die to get their hands on, not to mention the shitty pay scale when you work for the man. As a freelancer, you could charge what you want."

She snorted. "I'm not in this to get rich."

Crenel winked. "But you *are* in it to help people, and not just the people that you're *told* to help, the ones who need it. Go solo, and you can pick and choose. Charge the assholes through the nose and work pro-bono for the ones who can't find help anywhere else."

Penny snorted again. "That sounds highly unethical." Her brain ticked over his words, though. Having the freedom to get involved where she was needed, without having to rely on reams of paperwork to justify it?

Crenel nodded and stood. "Just think about it, okay?"

He left her alone, but the booth didn't stay that way for long. Cisco slid in next to her a few moments later, Red and Amelia taking the bench seat across from them.

"So, what about it?" Amelia asked, folding her hands on the table and leaning forward eagerly.

"What about what?" Penny asked, bewildered.

"We saw Crenel over here and guessed he gave you the same talk he gave all of us," Cisco explained. "FBI bad, free-lancing good, Mack will fund our little startup."

"Our what?" Penny laughed. "You guys have a whole business model planned already?"

"It's not like it was hard," Amelia protested. "You and Cisco are our field agents, I'll get the clients, and Red is our information guy. We've got all the skills we need. Trevor will come on in a few weeks as the tech guy. Dean March said he was supposed to graduate with us, but he accidentally fried the computer his extra credit assignments were on. It won't take him long to redo it, though."

Penny leaned back, dazed. She looked out into the thinning crowd that loitered at the bar and spotted Boots. She waved to the serpent, who hurried over. "Boots, these jobbers think we should start our own mythological investigative agency. What do you think?"

Boots looked at the faces peering down at her, then did

a happy twirl. She nodded eagerly, then shoved her entire head into Cisco's whiskey.

Penny laughed. "I guess that's a yes, but we might have to remind her in the morning. She's gonna be a little hungover, I bet."

THE END

I'm writing these notes on April 6. Yeah, Steve is gonna kill me.

This was my favourite book to write. It's home for me — albeit home with a magical twist — but between opening my new file to begin the story and right now, 'home' has changed. The whole world has.

I'm in quarantine with my family and oh my god there is not enough wine on the planet to make this work. I'm an introvert. There are FOUR PEOPLE in my house. And a dog. And they WON'T GO AWAY!* My only solace is the occasional outing with my friends. By 'friends' I mean my dog and my shiraz, and by 'outing' I mean my driveway.

How are you all doing? I know many of you are facing challenges so much bigger than mine. I hope you're all ok and that this book, and all the other authors are working so hard to get out, bring a sliver of brightness into a world that can be a little dark sometimes. I mean, look at Mike — he lives in Vegas and he can't even go out for ribs!

I'd like to thank you all (and Michael, as much as I give

him shit all the time) for helping my little series come to fruition. From 'write what you know… write YOU' so many months ago, to a rollicking adventure that has culminated in my very own backyard, I feel so blessed to have had this time with my new friend and her sassy snake.

It's the end of the series, but maybe not the end of Penny and Boots. We'll see. I've got other projects in the wings and they deserve their time to fly, too.

Love you all,

Amy.

(PS: Really, send wine. Lots of it. Help.)

THANK YOU for reading our story! We have a few of these planned, but we don't know if we should continue writing and publishing without your input. Options include leaving a review, reaching out on Facebook to let us know and smoke signals.

Frankly, smoke signals might get misconstrued as low hanging clouds so you might want to nix that idea...

Unlike Amy, I am not apologizing for writing these notes on the 7th of April... Probably way too late. Why? Because if I apologize then Steve will realize I really don't want to mess up the process and he might harass me a little more to get the author notes IN to him on time.

I have to keep him guessing. It's my job.

Like Amy, THANK YOU for reading along on these adventures and DO NOT MISS that Amy has a TON of other books available for you to read. Her humor is infectious, so read more!

Here is her website: https://amyhopkinsauthor.com

Diary

Unlike Amy, all of my kids are out of the house. So, in one way it is no different with the Coranavirus situation from a normal day without the children. In another, it is horrible.

They are grown adults, living on their own and I don't know what is going on with them at all.

Are they ok? Should I call? If they aren't ok is it a cold, is it something much worse?

Frankly, I do not have a warm fuzzy knowing exactly where they are, but I also don't struggle with young ones, which is a sword that cuts both ways.

I'm back from a mini-staycation looking at the massive buildings (Las Vegas) out my window that are closed.

I really wish they would let me go in and play, that would be amazing. I'd even write a story about their casino and they would become famous…er.

More famous.

What's not to like about that?

So, you know, anyone from MGM want to let me walk around the Veer (right next door) or MGM, NY NY?

No?

Dang.

Stay safe and healthy out there!

Michael Anderle

CONNECT WITH THE AUTHORS

Amy Hopkins Social
Website:
https://amyhopkinsauthor.com
Facebook:
https://www.facebook.com/thespellscribe

Michael Anderle Social
Website:
http://www.lmbpn.com

Email List:
http://lmbpn.com/email/

Facebook Here:
www.facebook.com/TheKurtherianGambitBooks/

www.ingramcontent.com/pod-product-compliance
Lightning Source LLC
Chambersburg PA
CBHW050258110726
47898CB00007B/2460